I0681239

THIRD SIDE
of the
COIN

———— ❧ ————

A Short Story Collection

Sarah Elisabeth Sawyer

Third Side of the Coin

© 2014 by Sarah Elisabeth Sawyer. All rights reserved.

RockHaven Publishing
P.O. Box 1103
Canton, Texas 75103
SarahElisabethWrites.com/RockHavenPublishing

Scripture taken from the New King James Version®. Copyright © 1982 by Thomas Nelson, Inc. Used by permission. All rights reserved.

Following are works of fiction. Names, characters, places, and incidents are fictitious or used fictitiously. Any resemblance to real persons, living or dead, is coincidental and unintentional.

Edited by Sarah Elisabeth Sawyer and Lynda Kay Sawyer

Interior Design: Sarah Elisabeth Sawyer

Cover Design: Josh McBride josh360.com

Author Photo by Kelly Blanchard

ISBN: 978-0-9910259-1-6
LCCN: 2014909570

What people are saying about Sarah Elisabeth Sawyer's writings…

"Really an extraordinary work. Compelling and warm…"
Aaron Morrow, author

"Your writing has a very comfortable flow to it."
Jackie Wilson, avid reader

"This comment is for your mom: Thank you for supporting your daughter as she spreads her wings and explores her gift of writing. I think you are represented by the color violet. A mix of proud-purple and love-red. :)"
Marita Thelander, multi-award winning author

"You have a gift for finding such creative and meaningful stories…"
Rachel Phelps, flash fiction master

"I'm one of your fans. I love how you create a truly dynamic story of depth, with a wholesome spiritual application."
Stanley Bednarz, writer

"Your storytelling voice is very sincere and allowed me to relax and enjoy…"
William Price, award winning Christian author

"You keep writing, you have a real gift."
Papaw (William Kenneth Odell)
Rest in Peace, April 2010

To my mama and daddy

CONTENTS

That's What Family is For

It Could Be Worse

Promoting
Christ-Centered Fine Arts

In *Third Side of the Coin* are stories of struggle and heartache. Nothing is wrapped in a pretty package tied with platitudes of living happily ever after. That's not reality. But just as there's despair, there's hope through Jesus Christ. Craft that message with excellence and we can touch a hurting soul.

Of the more than fifty inspirationally short stories I've written, *Apparently So* won the weekly FaithWriters.com Writing Challenge, and nine others received an Editor's Choice Award. I am in awe of the marvelous works the Lord does as I walk through the doors He opens.

For Him,
Sarah Elisabeth

I have seen your tears. Isa. 38:5

JOY COMES
IN THE MORNING

Everything

The sound of Maggie's footsteps reached his ears. John closed his laptop and clicked off the lamp. He stood and stepped away from his desk as the home office door opened to meet him. Maggie's face shone a ghostly white against the backdrop of the hall light. John looked past her.

The rasp in Maggie's voice grated his nerves. "Last minute revisions, John? I thought it was ready to send off. Getting cold feet?"

"No." John avoided brushing her as he moved through the doorway. "I'm going to bed. Have to get up early and work a job."

Maggie wasn't put off. "Sure, John, work, work. Write, write. What about us? When was the last time you actually talked to me?"

The scratch in her voice ground the edges of John's eardrum as she followed him down the hallway. Six months had passed since her last chemo treatment, but she hadn't fully recovered. He wished she'd stayed at her sister's house longer.

"I'm going to bed." John swung his hand behind him, closing the door of the guest bedroom with Maggie on the other side. He paused, expecting a follow-up tirade. Instead, he listened to her house shoes shuffling down the hall.

~~~

Sleep didn't come. Not anymore. The black hole of loss and heartache loomed close in the darkness of the night. John had considered filling it with alcohol, but he'd witnessed from his father how fruitless that proved. Only one thing kept his mind intact.

It only took a moment to retrieve his laptop from the office. The desktop was still running, his last Word doc filling the screen. He scrolled through his latest creation's dance of paragraphs. He smirked. Maggie thought he was working on the same manuscript. She didn't know the completed one lay in a manila envelope on the top shelf of the office closet, ready for mailing to his agent. He would skip lunch tomorrow and use the time for a trip to the post office.

He checked the clock. 2:16 a.m. His mind slipped into agonizing over how long it was until daylight, which caused his chest to burn. He crushed the thought and shifted his focus in the right direction–writing a masterpiece.

~~~

"Mornin', John. How's your wife?"

John grunted at Darrin as they clocked in. "She's okay."

"Any symptoms?"

"Symptoms?"

"Did the doctor say to watch for anything that might indicate...you know, that she might get sick again?"

"I guess. Her sister keeps up with it." John stepped into the side hall, muttering an excuse about needing to see someone. Anything to avoid walking with Darrin. The guy was way too cheerful to honestly exist in this sorry world, and he talked about God too much. Darrin had already hooked two guys in John's section, and he was starting to feel surrounded.

John set his phone's alarm for noon as he settled in his cubicle at the advertising company. He couldn't miss a minute of his lunch hour. He would dash to the car, drive downtown, grab the manila envelope from the backseat...

Wait. Was it in the backseat?

John swore under his breath as he visualized the bulky package lying on the coffee table. The memory played like a second-rate commercial. He'd laid the package down while he tied his shoe. Maggie called from the bedroom, asking if he'd left yet. He skipped tying the other one and hurried out the door, closing it soundlessly behind him. He'd left the manuscript behind.

~~~

When Darrin asked to join him for lunch, John's anger was still boiling.

Darrin spread his cold-cuts feast on the break room table. "What did you pack?"

"Nothing." John poured a mug of coffee and rattled the table with his descent into the chair next to Darrin.

"Good, 'cause my wife packed too much. You like turkey or beef?"

What I'd like is an extra half-hour to make a run home. If only I weren't already on the rocks with the boss. "Beef."

"How're your novel revisions coming?"

"They're done."

"Done? As in, ready for your agent to pitch?"

"Yeah."

"That's great, John! Congratulations."

The genuineness of Darrin's tone took John by surprise. He examined the man's face for the first time in the year and a half he'd known him. "Thanks. It's been a long project."

"I bet Maggie's excited."

John unwrapped the sandwich Darrin gave him. He wasn't in the habit of talking about his personal affairs. He didn't like people to know his business. But Darrin was—different. And John knew from the tightening of his own chest he'd better let out his frustrations to someone.

Around the chunk of sandwich he'd bit off, John said, "No, she's not. She hates my writing, constantly nags me about it. She'd love to see the manuscript I poured my guts in go up in flames. She's resented everything I've done since—" John tried to stuff the whole sandwich in his mouth. Even as he sat in the bright light of the break room, the dark hole opened up to consume him.

He jerked when Darrin said, "You know, darkness has to flee when it's exposed to the light of truth."

Beneath his sleeves, the hairs on John's arms prickled. How did Darrin know about the black hole?

The men sat in silence disrupted only by the crunch of potato chips. John fought against his next words until the strength to suppress them evaporated.

"Maggie and I tried for years to have children. She wanted a girl, I wanted a boy. We figured to have both eventually. When she got pregnant I figured life had finally begun.

Everything was about our child. We decorated the nursery room, studied potty training, picked out a college."

"But?" Darrin's pressure wasn't severe, but enough to force the pain from John's heart and out his mouth.

"She miscarried at eight months. She thinks I blame her, but I don't. I just couldn't stand the thought of going through it all again. Piled on top of everything else, that's what divided us. Guess we wouldn't still be together if she hadn't gotten cancer." John shrugged, thinking about the long nights home alone, Maggie in the hospital. He continued, "Since the miscarriage, this gigantic black hole in my mind swallows me up, day and night. Nothing helps, except writing. It's a safe way to live out my anger. Maggie says my stories are too bloody. I say it's better than the real blood I want to experience."

"Maybe real blood is what you need."

John stared into the empty chip bag. The black hole was everywhere.

Darrin's words finally registered. "What kind of crazy talk is that?"

"Not crazy, John. I'm talking about real blood. Forgiveness. Hope. Peace. Jesus Christ shed His blood on the cross for all those things. There is power in His blood to wash away sins. To heal you. Power to give you *life*, John. Life. All you have to do is receive it."

The lunch hour stretched to two.

~~~

"Maggie, I'm home!" John tripped over the suitcase planted in front of the door. He touched the cool plastic handle before sidestepping it as he entered the living room. "Maggie?"

His eyes went to the coffee table—not in search of his manila envelope but rather the sight of their wedding album hanging half over the edge. Soft footsteps brought his attention to the doorway of the hall. He hadn't realized how drawn Maggie's face had become. The cancer ordeal had taken much of the lively, beautiful girl he had married. Or maybe he'd done this to her.

"Maggie, I have something to tell you."

The thin wisp of her lips moved with definition. "And I have something to tell you." Maggie dropped her burden of a bulging duffle bag to the floor. The thud sent a chill down John's spine. "We've been married for thirteen years. I can't count the things you've had your way. I don't know why we've stayed together this long, but I'm correcting that mistake now." She picked up the bag and moved into the living room. John watched her, his heart beginning to pound. She wouldn't really leave him—would she?

"Maggie, listen. That's why I came straight home. I know what a failure I've been as a husband, as a man. That's all changing as of right now. God changed me. I gave my heart to Jesus Christ. I'm not angry anymore. I—"

"Wonderful to hear." Maggie shoved their wedding album to the floor with one hand. The manila envelope lay exposed, accusing. "I'm glad you're no longer angry with me for something I didn't do. That's makes everything peachy."

John felt like he was clawing his way up a hill of oil. "I'm sorry, Maggie. I never meant—"

Maggie jerked around to stare at him, and her voice jumped to its highest pitch. "Sorry? Oh please, do you really think an apology will solve anything? Where were you while I was going through chemo, throwing up? How many times did you hold my hand those long nights in the hospital? For crying out loud, I had to recover at my sister's house because you claimed you wouldn't be able to take care of me. But we both know the truth."

Maggie picked up the thick package containing John's source of release for so many years. She strangled it as her tears flowed. "Here it is. This is the child we never had. Your lover. Everything you wanted in life I tried to give you and failed. It's all you need."

She shoved the manuscript into John's chest. The action caved it in. "Maggie, please, there's still a chance—"

"For what? Our marriage?" Maggie bent over and riffled through the scattered wedding pictures. She held out one of the joyful bride and groom. "Some things in life can be fixed, John. But some things can't."

Maggie's trembling fingers ripped the photo in half. "Our marriage is one thing that can't."

~ ~ ~

When Maggie's sister, Sandy, arrived in her blue Camry, John helped load the five bags. He added a few other things he thought his wife might need: the desktop computer, a bottle of multivitamins, and her favorite pillow.

The three avoided small talk. John closed the trunk and stepped back, watching as Sandy helped his wife into the passenger seat. Maggie didn't wave good-bye. Neither did he.

Back inside the tomb-like house, John stood in the middle of the living room and waited. The black hole was coming. He could feel it to the tips of his fingers, sucking him down. He raked a hand through his hair. His heart exploded.

John strode to the fireplace that hadn't produced the aroma of smoke in years. With a vicious shriek, he raked photo frames and knick-knacks from the mantle. They crashed to the hearth, shattering. He grabbed the cream colored ceramic lamp and slung it across the room. Its cord jerked from the outlet, halting the flight and landing it with a dull breaking sound. He grabbed the manuscript from the rubble and twisted it in his hands.

Dropping to his knees, John demanded, "God, help me."

Silence followed. John waited to be lost forever in the black hole. The only place he belonged. Thoughts of his hunting rifle in the hall closet attacked his mind.

Beams from the setting sun filtered through the blinds and across the floor. John's eyes fixed on the pieces of the torn wedding photo. He knew the next step to take. Somehow, he had to believe God would show him the one after that.

After placing a few pieces of tape along the back of the photo, John scanned it and printed a full color copy. He gazed at the two happiest people in the world. That's what they said back then.

If only he could piece his marriage back together as easily.

The phone rang. John shook his head as the caller ID flashed. He let the answering machine pick up.

The voice sounded annoyed. "Hey John, it's Brad. I need your manuscript in my office by like yesterday. We've worked hard on lining things up, and it's time to move. Get it to me A-sap."

John sat on the floor among the broken ceramic, and leaned against the couch. He watched the sun go down. "Okay, God. I gave everything over to you and my wife left me. Is that a sign You're really going to work me over for all the junk I've done in my life? That's not what Darrin said. Guess he was wrong. Guess I was wrong about this whole God thing."

Another hour passed and the phone rang again. John fumbled for it and glanced at the caller ID. His pulse quickened as the number exploded fireworks in his eyes. *Sandy.* Perhaps Maggie...

His voice cracked. "Hello? Maggie?" The silence on the other end lingered long enough for John's heart rhythm to slow.

"No, it's Sandy."

John licked his dry lips. "How's Maggie?"

A loud snort told him Sandy was trying to blow her nose. Her nasal tone said she must've cried hard. "She didn't want me to call, but you should know. She's in the hospital. The cancer's back and the doctor says she won't beat it this time."

~~~

John knocked on the door of room 716. He tried not to think about how the fragrance of the flowers he held reminded him of a funeral.

"Come in."

Why had he scoffed at Maggie's hoarse voice? He should walk away and never look back. Maggie could never forgive him. His actions were beyond it.

I forgive you. Forgive yourself. Then let Maggie make her decision.

Despite the confidence he lacked in that quiet voice, John pushed the door open.

Maggie's expression spoke volumes. "I told Sandy—"

"Don't be mad at her, Maggie. I'm not staying long. Just wanted to bring you a few things."

"What, your manuscript for me to read one final time?"

John stared at the flowers for a moment. The words slipped out. "I erased it from the computer and burned the last copy."

Maggie's gasp shot through the distance between them. "But that was your dream."

One step at a time, John moved to his wife's bedside, set the vase of red roses on the side table and laid a Bible next to it. He reached for her hand, but she moved it away.

He couldn't meet her eyes. "*You* are my dream, Maggie. Nothing comes before you now, except God. It's because of Him I'm able to do that. I can't on my own. I guess you know that well enough." John tapped the Bible cover with his finger. "I have a new story to write now."

Maggie lifted her chin as a tear slid off it. "Sounds intrigue-ing. But—it's too late for us."

John shook his head, and raised his eyes to hers. "I know I've hurt you bad, Maggie. More than anyone should have to forgive. I'm willing to wait as long as it takes to earn your trust again."

Tears poured from Maggie's eyes as she rolled them to the ceiling. "There's not enough time left."

He flipped open the front cover of the Bible and lifted his repaired version of their wedding photo.

"Some things just can't be fixed. But some things can." He held the photo in her view, and then slipped it into the bou-quet of roses. "With God's help, our marriage is one thing that can."

Maggie shifted her gaze to him. The deep well of her green eyes flooded his heart as he thumbed away her tears. John moved his hand to lightly take hers, and she allowed it. His heart skipped a beat.

Secure

A finger burying its way into her back jolted Helen awake. The whisper echoed in her ear. "I think someone's in the kitchen."

Helen clicked on her bedside lamp and rolled to face her granddaughter, Beth. The fifteen-year-old scooted away, the patchwork quilt tucked under her chin. Helen nodded. "Do you want to come with me to make sure everything's locked? Might help you sleep better."

Beth shook her head, eyes focused on the sheets.

Helen sent up a silent prayer. "I'll go see."

Robe slung over her shoulders, Helen ignored her house shoes as she trudged to the bedroom door. She managed to have her eyes fully open by the time she reached the kitchen. She flipped the light and checked the back door, though she knew it hadn't been tampered with. No crime in her neighborhood for thirty years. The only recent incident in the town with a population of twelve hundred had been kids shoplifting candy at the lone grocery store. Nothing like the city Beth had run away from.

Helen moved to the window. She wanted to be able to tell Beth she had checked everything.

Fourth night in a row. First the living room. Then the enclosed back porch. Last night, the attic. Though Helen didn't care how many nights she had to check the house in order to sooth Beth's fears, the lack of sleep wore on her aged body.

The first night Beth came to stay with her, the girl locked herself in the guest bedroom. After the second night, Helen offered to let Beth sleep with her, which she refused. The third night, after Helen roamed the attic, she returned to bed to find Beth in it, eyes wide and staring out in space.

Kitchen secure, Helen made her way through the living room to the front door. Only five days ago she learned her grandchild had run away from home. A day later, she received the call from a social worker, asking Helen to house the teen. Beth's mom, Helen's daughter, was in jail on drug possession charges. Beth, whom Helen had not seen since age six, was at a hospital receiving post-rape care.

The dead bolt, never used until this week, rested in place. Another prayer sent up, Helen turned lights off as she made her way back to the bedroom.

She paused at the guestroom. All of her daughter's childhood belongings were stored in its closet. A memory vaulted to Helen's weary mind. She entered the room.

Minutes later, she returned to her own bedroom and found Beth staring in space again. Helen held a stuffed animal close to her heart, and sat on the edge of the bed next to her granddaughter. She wished she were allowed to brush the wild strands of auburn hair from Beth's eyes.

Helen pinched her lips, staying off the tears. "Everything's locked down tight."

Beth remained emotionless.

Helen lifted the stuffed animal, a brown and white dog, into Beth's view. She wiggled it back and forth to make his ears wave. "Your mom called him Floppy. Kept him in bed with her every night 'til she was seventeen. Said Floppy was her guard dog."

No response. Helen laid the soft-coated toy by Beth's arm and stood. Moving around to the other side of the bed, she turned the lamp off and slipped in next to Beth. A distance greater than the king-sized mattress wedged between them.

Sleep had drifted close when Helen heard the voice whispering again. It rang with doubt. "You're praying for me, aren't you?"

Helen throttled her tears. "Every waking moment."

Silence. Then, "Grandma?"

"Yes, Baby Girl?"

"If it sounds like someone's in the house again, I'm going with you to look. I think I'll sleep better."

In the moonlight, Helen could see Floppy pressed against Beth's cheek, his worn fur absorbing her tears.

Forgotten

God has forgotten me.

This revelation sought me out gradually. It began the day I could no longer turn over in bed.

"Good morning, Ms. Ruth. How are we feeling today?"

I liked when my nurse, Karen, patted my shoulder. Her gentle touch soothed when she lifted or bathed me. She recognized me as a person. I once could see her smile, but I've lost that. I can no longer see past the foot of my bed. Now Karen has vanished from my life, replaced by a nurse who doesn't see me.

God has forgotten me.

The fact didn't come in a reverberating crack from the heavens. It didn't come with any sound at all. Days and years drained my senses to a trickling stream. My failed hearing could scarce discern the tone of a voice, and dumbness had long since sabotaged my tongue. No one pats my shoulder or speaks to me when they administer a shot or change my bedding. They have forgotten I'm still inside this withering shell.

So has God.

I will never know an answered prayer again. I am left with nothing to do but breathe. In. Out. In. Out. I cling to the hope of taking the next breath as my last.

Sometimes I wish for enough vision to see the framed photos covering the far wall. Images of loved ones in my mind's eye has blurred and faded. They live so far away. The children in the pictures now have children I've never met. The last years have brought few visitors. They've forgotten I'm still alive. *So has God.*

I breathe. Another night drags into morning.

A squeaky voice fills the drainage in my ear. I struggle to focus on the speaker. Dried sleep in the corners of my eyes makes the battle painful. Young faces crowd near my bed and one child slides something onto the medicine cart constant by my side.

"Merry Christmas!" the voices sing out.

Christmas? I breathe and grunt a reply. They stand near enough for me to see their uncertain expressions at the gurgle of my sucking inhale. They wave as each backs out of my vision range. All but one.

She looks young. No more than twelve, if such youth is still possible. She steps close to my side and extends her hand to cover mine. She squeezes with the tenderness found between mother and infant.

The warmth from her hand flows through my body and tingles down to my toes. She speaks; I catch bits of her sentence.

"My name i…Cindy. I saw o…the label th…you're Ruth Anderson. I hope it…okay t…call you Ms. Ruth." She stops, and I fear she will leave. I don't want her to release my hand.

With all my concentration, I find enough strength to squeeze with two fingers. Cindy smiles and begins to circle her thumb over the wrinkles of my spotty skin. The action bunches it together then smoothes it out as fine as a baby's. I almost forget to breathe. My chest vibrates with the effort.

"…need t…catch up with the oth…Ms. Ruth. But first is i…okay if…pray with you?"

Her study of my face stirs my heart to life. Perhaps she searches for signs of comprehension. I struggle to show with my eyes what my tongue cannot say.

Our eyes connect, and Cindy nods her head before bowing it. "Dear God I lif…Ms. Ruth up to you. I don't know wh… she faces everyday bu…You do. I pray th…You will meet her needs. Lord, please help her know th…You have not forgotten her and th…why you sent us here today, i…Jesus name, amen."

As Cindy squeezes my hand, pats my shoulder, and promises to visit me again, I realize breathing is not the only thing I can still do. I can cry.

Red Light Thoughts

Alice counted the white stripes as they flashed by, noted the early morning joggers on the concrete path circling the lake. Checked her speedometer, observed the light traffic in her rearview mirror. She had to keep her mind occupied every second. It wasn't easy, even though her drive to work was short. But distractions were plentiful to fill all the little spaces—until she hit the red light.

Her mind slowed with her car tires and tension assaulted her stomach muscles. Surely there was something interesting she could think about, something at the intersection to hone in on. But no. Thoughts held at bay thus far had the upper hand and they released with overwhelming fury.

Oh please, did you really believe you'd get away with a peaceful drive to work? You don't deserve that. In fact, things are better than you deserve. What a loser you are. You'll never have peace. Your past is right on your bumper and there's no escape.

Looking for something to distract me? Try that garbage can on the corner. A perfect analogy of your life. All the rotten trash accumulated in its rightful place. You. Always trashing everything you touch.

Alice sucked for air. Only five more minutes and the stresses of work would drown the voice burying her in guilt. If only that light would change. The longest light in town, and it just happened to be on her daily route.

Of course you're in a hurry to get to work. Those people in the check-out line are dying to see your ugly face. And your co-workers? Well, we all know what they think of you. Ha, imagine what they'd think if they knew you were a so-called Christian. You should try witnessing to them. Your life would confirm what a lousy choice it is.

A squeal of rubber sounded as Alice pealed out with the green light. She shot through the intersection and continued accelerating. Then she spotted the blue and red lights flashing in her rearview mirror.

See? Total loser.

~~~

"Mommy, come here."

Alice checked her watch. "No, Casey, I have to get ready for work and you're about to catch the bus. Put your shoes on." She slipped her arms in the mauve sweater and caught a last look at her appearance in the full length mirror hung from the back of her bedroom door.

You're nothing but a homely little—

"Come on, Casey." Alice opened the door to her daughter's room and lost it. "Casey! You're not even dressed! You'll make me late if you miss the bus. Get changed right now." Alice snatched the colored pencil from the pajama clad seven-year-old's hand and pointed to the closet. "Now."

A tear trickled down Casey's cheek as she turned away.

Alice dropped her eyes to the floor where the evidence of a busy morning was scattered. Crayons and papers covered two thirds of the tiny space. The one Casey had been working on caught her eye. She bent and picked it up. A house with two girls in front, one small with blonde hair, the other larger with brown hair. Scribbled under the picture were the words: *i wan be mommy.*

Alice didn't try to beat the red light. In fact, she was glad to be caught in silence. She deserved the thought lashing.

What kind of mother are you? Yelling at your little girl, making her cry just because she was coloring. Is there no end to your shame? Good grief, she's a seven-year-old! And of all things—she was coloring a picture for you. She wants to be just like her mommy. What a nightmare!

Oh, and just for the record—you will never win the battle over your tongue. It's a fire stick and someday it will start the blaze that's going to burn your whole world down around your ears. Wait and see.

A blaring car horn started Alice in motion again as she crept through the intersection, tears streaking her makeup. She was no better than a criminal that should be in prison. Wait. She already was.

~~~

The red light routine became a comforting one. Sit still for two minutes and let the truth be told.

You are an utter failure. Why don't you tattoo it on your forehead? Oh yeah, it is. Two time divorcee. What good Christian gets a divorce? Sure, the first was before your so-called Salvation. But what about the other? You loused it up with your sorry self. And you know what? God knows it. You failed Him. He is finished with you. You're just no good to anyone. Give it up.

Alice's breathes came in short gasps. Her vision darkened, and pain shot through her chest. The red light beamed at her like a consuming fire.

You're worthless. You—

"Be quiet!" Alice gripped the steering wheel until her knuckles whitened. "Stop it. Please help me, Lord." Her voice shook, but she pushed the words through her lips. "I renounce these lies from Satan in the name of Jesus and by the power of His blood. I am a forgiven child of God, covered by His grace and mercy. By faith I will overcome."

You really think praying will help—

"Get behind me, Satan!" Alice sat up in her seat, mind focused. "You have no place in my heart or my mind."

It's not that easy—

"I declare all your works defeated in Jesus' name." The light flashed to green. Alice checked her rearview. With no vehicles in sight, she slouched in her seat, foot still planted on the brake. The silence drifted in one ear and out the other—uninterrupted.

"Thank You, Lord," she whispered. "Thank You."

Don't stop here, child. A kind, soft voice spoke not in her mind, but her spirit. *Continue to renounce the voice of condemnation, but then replace those thoughts with Me.*

Fragments of scripture flowed through her mind and out her mouth. "Whatever things are pure, lovely, just, a good report, praiseworthy—think on these things...Bring every thought into captivity...I have loved you with an everlasting love."

The light turned red again, but no tension assaulted Alice. She relaxed and glanced at the car braking to a halt alongside her. The man drummed his hand on the steering wheel and lifted his wristwatch. He stared at the red light.

Months passed, and though her self-talk still tried to barrel in some mornings, Alice found with her commitment to memorize a new scripture verse each day, there simply was no room for lies.

Satiety

Sand gritted in the spaces between my teeth. Swollen tongue pasted to the roof of my mouth, I plunged to the floor of the swirling desert.

A voice wafted through the air. No, it could not be. I had run too far; surely I must be long beyond the reach of anyone. My lolling tongue tasted the dust as laughter forced its way through at the irony. Beyond reach is where I had wanted to be. I should congratulate myself.

A vulture's screech brought me to my feet as I looked to the circle of birds gathering above me.

"You can't!" I screamed. "You can't! I wasn't promised death. I was promised—"

My tongue absorbed the raw sensation of blood seeping from my lip. I plodded on, eyes darting to the horrific creatures again and again.

I was sure the voice called out. He still followed me.

When I crested the top of a sand dune, my eyes captured

the valley below. Lush greenery adorned the entrance of a lovely garden, its centerpiece a lake of sparkling diamonds.

Overwhelmed with thirst, I tumbled from the dune and through a rose covered arbor, landing within inches of my passion. Scooping my hand through the chillingly clear water, I lifted it to my lips. The voice called again, causing the liquid to spill from my vibrating palm.

"Leave me alone!" I tried to sound authoritative and in control, but I knew my weak tremor was pathetic.

I had to drink *now*. But as I reached for the crystal lovely-ness, my eyes caught something they were blind to at first. Thousands upon thousands of moaning humans lay scattered among heaps of skulls and bones lining the shore around the lake.

My eyes traveled the full circle of the incredible sight, finally resting on an agonized face I recognized, a friend. One who had persuaded me to take this journey. Why was he here?

"Drink it." His voice was a whisper as he spoke around the bulk in his mouth. "Drink it. It's good. It'll make you happy."

I hesitated. My eyes moved past his prone position to the corpses around him. He grabbed my throat and hissed, "Drink it!" His mouth opened wider, and I saw the gravel that filled it as his body convulsed. The grip loosened and his last breath evaporated.

Looking around for the lushness surrounding the lake, I saw nothing but wide boards propped up by scrap wood. Fake. All fake with the exception of the poisoned water that had captured these lives.

Fear overcoming thirst, I crashed through the cardboard arbor, desperate to flee death. But the bitter taste filling my mouth became a constant reminder of my doom. There was no escape.

Knees buckling, I fell on my face as images flashed through my mind. A variety of sensations saturated my tongue. The crude oil of lust. The acidic tang of forgiveness denied. The chalky dust of hatred. The rusty erosion of selfishness. They overwhelmed me until I longed to cut out my tongue and be free from the satiety of flavors I had sought vehemently in this desert. To what end?

Vultures waited in their patient circle.

The voice called again. I comprehended the words. Rather the one word, repeated.

He called my name.

No. He had nothing to offer I could accept. *Please don't find me.*

"Child."

The voice was so close I only had to lift my head and behold Him. But I couldn't.

A splash of water bathed my face. My tongue screamed for it; anything to wash the bile away. The gentle coolness of a cup neared my lips. I dared to meet His eyes.

"I can't. I—I don't deserve it."

The cup touched my lips. "You will die without it."

They were simple words, pure. True. I nodded.

He cradled my head as life from His cup poured through the bitter sand that filled my mouth. The water gushed in, but the sand did not wash out. It dissolved as the source of my deliverance rushed through my entire being.

The water was alive. So was I.

Bread gained by deceit [is] sweet to a man, But afterward his mouth will be filled with gravel. Pro. 20:17 (NKJV)

"He who believes in Me, as the Scripture has said, out of his heart will flow rivers of living water." John 7:38 (NKJV)

Scarred

Melissa made a left into the apartment's parking lot and checked her door locks a third time. She strained to see through the dimly lit entryway, its own windows covered in bars. No sign of Angie. She frowned and checked the illuminated numbers on her dashboard. The rain had made her five minutes late, but Angie wouldn't have left. Melissa sighed. It was more likely Angie hadn't been waiting for her at all.

After parking as close to the one security light as possible, Melissa dashed through the drizzle to the apartment entrance. The bars were ironic since the door itself was never locked, even at night. She skipped every other step to ascend the stairs to the third floor. Her thoughts fell in rhythm with her brisk pace.

Give her time…she looks up to you…don't crush her spirit…she's kicked some major stuff…go easy on her…

Melissa wasn't sure if the self-talk was a prayer or the cautioning voice of the Lord, but she needed it. Her own patience wouldn't last.

It took four rings on the bell and a steady tap-tap on the door of apartment 308 before Angie cracked it open. She was in her bathrobe, locks of died black hair dangling over her shoulders. Melissa looked at her wristwatch then back at Angie.

Angie swiped untrimmed bangs from her eyes and spoke through one side of her lips. "Look, Melissa, I know I said I'd go with ya tonight, but I've had this terrible headache all day…"

"Can I at least come in?"

Angie's hesitancy was pointed, but Melissa wasn't about to back down. Angie pushed the door away from her as she leaned on the jamb and waved her hand. "Why not?"

Melissa took the few steps to the couch, which was propped at one end with a crushed beer can. The smell of cigarette smoke would never come out of those cushions. She cleared a spot to sit among the *Help Wanted* sections of every publication in the city.

Angie's descent onto the couch made the survival of the remaining legs nothing short of miraculous. Melissa watched the disheveled younger woman grab a pack of cigarettes and thump one out. Everything she said would affect Angie's life—for better or worse. Still, there was no way around her typical straightforward approach. Ask the hard questions. Shut up and listen.

"Why won't you come to the ladies fellowship?"

Angie lit the cigarette and retrieved a ponytail holder from the pocket of her bathrobe. Hair gathered behind her head, she snapped the band on the second twist. "I wanted to, Mel. Really. When you helped me find Jesus, I—I can't even describe it. It was like someone breathing life into me. I wanted to know all about everything. But when you took me to your church last Sunday, I dunno." She shrugged. "Even cleaned up and in a dress, I felt funny, like everyone probably knew all I'd done. I didn't want to go back, but I was going to until…"

The tumble of words halted. Melissa noticed the traces of tears on Angie's cheeks. *Lord, she's come so far in only two weeks. Am I pushing too hard?*

She knew caution was key, but she sensed the ice solid enough to bear treading. "Until what?"

Angie's sigh still sounded like a hiss. She deposited her half-burnt cigarette in the coffee table ashtray and yanked on the sleeve of her robe, drawing it to her elbow. "I was getting dressed and look. You can see them a mile away." Angie shook her head enough for her restrained hair to whip her cheeks. "How can I shake those ladies hands with these staring at them?"

Not an easy thing to look at, not by far. But as Melissa stroked the scars with a finger, she saw them differently. "What did you feel when you did this?"

Angie's eyes went to the shag carpet and she shrugged her thin shoulders. "I don't know. Just high."

"What do you feel now when you see the needle tracks?"

"Ashamed. Worthless. Stupid." Angie tugged her sleeve back in place and reached for her cigarette, letting it dangle between her fingers.

"You know what I see?" Melissa brushed a straggling tear from her own cheek. "I see sins forgiven. Mercy shown. They're evidence of the unconditional love of Christ." She reached for the sleeve, sliding it up again. "Heroin tracks. That's what they were. But you know what they are now?" Melissa traced a bluish line with her thumb. "Reminders of

God's grace."

The cigarette slipped from Angie's fingers and fell on the shag carpet. She retrieved it and tossed the butt in the ashtray. Her eyes went back to her scar-covered arm. "You're right, Mel. Thanks."

~~~

It would be three long years before Melissa was privileged to witness Angie give her testimony before a congregation of over five hundred at a woman's retreat.

"She doesn't care for recognition," Angie began, "But I could not tell this story without talking about my sister, Melissa. I'm so thankful for her tough love. She helped me realize several important things those first few weeks and months when I wouldn't leave my apartment, much less get a job. One of my best decisions was to move in with her. She made me realize home was the best place to start over." Angie's voice cracked and Melissa looked away. Choosing to sit on the front row had not been wise. There would be no chance of them making it through this with eyes connected.

A moment passed before Melissa could watch Angie pull up the sleeve of her flower pattern blouse. "I still have the scars from when I used drugs. I thought they would be a constant reminder of how it felt to get high and what a wreck I'd made of my life. But my sister shed some light on this. Now when I look at them, I'm reminded of the greatness of God's grace and just how far He's brought me. I feel a rush like no other. Trust me; I've been on both sides. And I'm here to testify as to which is the true high."

Tissue in hand, Melissa dried the tears that fell on her own scarred arm.

Twisted Hope

Silence clogged the air of the empty house. Sean grabbed the remote, dropped into his recliner and flipped on the TV. He changed the channel and swore. "Propaganda masquerading as cartoons."

Again.

"Killing for no reason."

Again.

"Love without relationship."

And again. His fingers tightened around the control. "The ultimate—people talking about God who have no idea what a monster He is." Sean hurled the remote at the screen, shattering it.

So much for humanity.

~~~

They used to have good times, Sean and his literary agent,

Jeff. Golf, bowling, or a Saturday night movie with the wives. But as Jeff sat behind the desk across from him, Sean knew more than a hunk of oak furniture separated them. Jeff's head was bent at a painful angle, his bald spot pronounced as he scanned his notes for the sixth time.

Sean refused to fill the air with small talk. It wasn't until Jeff sighed, lifted his head and shoved his glasses up for an eye massage that Sean spoke. "No good, huh?"

Jeff dropped his hands. "You know better. I don't spend three weeks evaluating a manuscript, then toss it back with 'no good.' I got a lot more to say."

"I don't want to hear it."

"Then find another agent."

With the way things had been lately, Sean couldn't be sure Jeff was bluffing. "I know what you're going to say."

"Then *you* say it."

Sean maintained eye contact. "You think it's too depressing."

Jeff slumped back against his chair, making the whole thing rock. "Sean, you've been my friend a long time. My client even longer. I'm talking to you now as an agent.

"You built an incredible setting, and made me connect with your protagonist in ways I never want anyone to know. You had me near tears yet ready to pull up my bootstraps. Then poof! He dies alone one night. Senselessly. Alone. No epiphany, no hope. No point."

Sean anchored himself in the cushion-less wood chair. "That *is* the point. There's no hope for a homeless guy no one sees. Who cares how many die every year?" Sean let a significant pause linger, then added, "My guy's only hope is death."

Jeff's chair rocked to an upright position as he stood, took off his glasses and folded them. In three steps he seated himself on the front of his desk, moving from agent to friend. His eyes stayed on the folded glasses in his hand. "Sean, I know how hard it's been since Jeanette—passed away. But she wouldn't want this. She was a woman of faith—"

"Leave my personal life out of it," Sean said, rising unconsciously and standing too close to Jeff's tense position.

Jeff cocked his head up to meet Sean's glare. "Can you?"

Something inside Sean broke, slid into his gut and exploded. His fist balled and drew back, but he checked himself. Taking a step back, Sean tripped on the cushion-less chair before turning to stride out the door. Jeff's grunt stopped him.

"Hit the streets, Sean. Find the inspiration that started you writing ten years ago."

~~~

Sean knew Jeff hadn't meant for him to take the advice literally. But he did.

At the corner of Valley and Lone Oak, the busiest intersection in the city, Sean leaned over a trash can that reeked almost as bad as he did. He retrieved a recently used Styrofoam cup, and slung out the remaining coffee grounds before positioning himself between two newspaper racks. The cup extended a foot away from his body, he tucked his other hand in the pocket of the Goodwill jacket he'd smeared with ketchup and ink. Frost in the January air numbed his fingertips and toes.

A man, bundled in a black trench coat, dropped quarters in the cup.

From behind a high red collar, a woman hissed, "Get a job."

In less than an hour, Sean had all the inspiration he could

stomach. Time to find a new agent.

Crushing the cup in his fist, he shoved his way through the human traffic and entered the alley where he'd parked his car. This world deserved to hear how rotten and hopeless they were, and that if God didn't care, no one else should either.

Sean heard the clumping footfall behind him before a flat surface landed between his shoulder blades. He staggered against the trunk of his Buick and turned in time to grasp the wrist thrusting a solid edge alongside his ribcage.

"Gimme the keys!" The words sprayed into Sean's face from a mouth filled with yellowed and gapped teeth.

The strength of the maniac surprised Sean as he tried to shove him away. If not for the trunk bending his spine in two, Sean would be flat on the ground. He twisted the maniac's wrist as a new voice added to the fray.

"Get off!"

The face of someone grabbing the maniac's shoulders appeared and pulled him back. In the jerk, Sean spun and dropped to his knees. He stumbled to his feet, preparing to land more than one fair punch, but the maniac's clumping stride had already sent him to the end of the alley, disappearing from sight.

Air seething between his teeth, Sean nodded to the young man standing before him, who offered a supporting hand on his arm. No gratitude warmed his heart, but Sean managed, "You just saved my life."

The other shook his head, shaggy brown hair fluffing out. "Eddy didn't know what he was doing, just that he wanted to take your car for a joyride."

Sean jerked his arm away. "Jabbing a knife at my gut meant that maniac had more than joyriding on his mind."

The soft chuckle raised hairs on the back of Sean's neck

and he wanted to pop the kid's mouth—until he held out the knife and said, "Can't do much with no blade. You want it?"

Sean worked his jaw to keep from snapping the kid's head off. He slapped his hand down on the open palm, met the unaffected eyes of the other, and wrapped his fingers around the bladeless knife. "Thanks for taking care of any fingerprints. I'm still turning it over to the police and see that maniac put behind bars."

"He was wearing gloves."

The kid was way too calm and collected. "Maybe I'll just take you to the police. You seem to know quite a bit."

The young man bent to retrieve a backpack from the ground and slung it over one shoulder. "No more than anyone else around here."

"Meaning what?"

"Meaning I have to be going. Got a long walk yet before dark." He started to turn away.

"Wait a second!" Sean studied the other from head to toe. His denim jacket with holes in each elbow covered a dirty black t-shirt. They matched the hole spotted jeans and soiled tennis shoes. The kid must do a fair amount of that walking. "What's your name?"

"David."

No last name offered. Sean straightened. "How do you know *I'm* not a cop?"

The young man coughed and covered his mouth, but not before Sean saw the amused smile. "You're too clumsy."

Sean let the comment slide, and jumped to his next question, the old journalism nature taking over. "Where'd you come from?"

"I could ask you the same. You're no bum. Why dress like one?"

"My question first."

David grinned. "Aren't you just glad I showed up when I did?"

The bantering grinded Sean's nerves. If he didn't owe this kid his life, he'd deck him. "I'm taking you to the police station, and you're going to tell them everything."

Another step back, but David kept his smile. No anger, no hard line. In fact, his clear face shined. "Can't. But tell you what—drive on down to the big red brick building at the end of the street. You'll find what you need." He swung his backpack down to his other hand and unzipped it. "You're gonna need this." He handed Sean a small paperback book.

Sean wanted to grab the kid's wrist and put him on the ground, but just stood still with the book in hand. With a small wave, David disappeared down the alley.

A quick jerk opened the driver's side door and Sean dropped behind the steering wheel, relocking the doors. He waited until the blasting heat from the vents produced feeling in his fingers before moving the gearshift to drive.

Sean parallel parked in front of his destination, hot acid filling his chest. A church. A place he'd sworn to curse until the day he died.

Jeanette had liked to drag him along with her to church every Sunday. He never complained; some of his novels were even inspired by a sermon or struggling parishioner. But now, everything about church spoke of his past, of what he'd lost. What God stripped away.

He lifted his foot off the brake. The flashing neon sign from the bar down the street offered more solutions than this place.

But for reasons he couldn't explain to himself, he passed it and made a u-turn at the light.

Minutes later, Sean leaned against the cold sleekness of his car, staring at the big red brick building. He'd parked on the opposite side, a sense of security at having four lanes of traffic between him and the church.

This was stupid. What answers could it possible hold? Maybe it housed homeless people. He could see up close and personal the despair in those people's eyes and know without doubt—faith gave nothing but false hope.

As he stared at the building, his mother's soft words whispered to his spirit. *I know you're hurting, son. I am too. But God's still watching over us.* That was after his dad was killed in a car accident. His mom hadn't been there when he buried Jeanette. She already rested by his father.

There had to be answers. Sean strode through the cross-walk and up the wide front steps. He yanked open one of the glass double doors, letting it bang before it could slowly follow him to a close.

All-too-familiar odors of carpet and wood pews served to prelude the sight of a few people sitting in them. They stared at the altar or perhaps the stain glass above it. The piece depicted Jesus holding a lamb.

The click of a door closing turned Sean like a soldier. A suit clad man approached him, hand outstretched. "Welcome. I'm Pastor James." Sean ignored the simple greeting and offered hand as he waited for a sermon. None came. They stared at each other a moment.

Sean cleared his throat. "Do you know David?"

"Yes, I do. One of the finest young men you could know."

Sean crossed his arms. "Where does he live?"

Pastor James swept an arm around to indicate the front door. "Everywhere. He's a street kid."

"What?" Arms dropping to his side, Sean regretted not

keeping the surprise out of his voice. It wasn't possible. No street kid smiled like that.

"He's not an ordinary one. I don't know much about his background, but I do know he loves the Lord, and he'd tell you about Jesus Christ even if you had a gun between his eyes."

Sean held desperately to the broken glass of his heart, skin breaking and blood flowing. Yet the glass slipped through his fingers.

He turned from the pastor, wanting him to walk away, and sank into the nearest pew. The pastor put a hand on his shoulder. Sean heard him praying. He stared at the small paperback he realized he'd been holding. Had the pastor seen it?

Sean lifted his head again, searching for the presence of so many he could feel. He thumb-fanned the thin pages of the book, sending a spray of scents to awaken him. Winter, the streets, his car. His thumb stopped on a marked corner with a highlighted passage.

For God so loved the world that He gave His only begotten Son, that whoever believes in Him should not perish but have everlasting life.

Sean's own words echoed back to him: *"His only hope is death."*

Two hours later, Sean called Jeff. "We need to talk."

This Isn't Funny

I don't know why I agreed to let my sister, Sandra, drag me to her ladies' Bible thingy. Meeting new people isn't high on my wish list, but here I sit in the circle of sweet faces, all looking at me. The leader, Angie, asks something else from her memorized let's-get-to-know-you questionnaire. "What does your husband do? His name is Mark, right?"

"He's a comedian."

That strikes a chord, as usual. Everyone laughs.

Angie says, "Ha, so is mine."

"No, I mean, that's what he does for a living." If you can call it that. Our living isn't so good. I tug on the edges of my frayed miniskirt, and endure the typical response after the awkward pause.

"Oh. Well, that must be fun!"

I just smile and nod. I didn't come to embarrass Sandra, who sits beside me. I'm counting on tapping her for forty dollars to pay the gas bill from two months ago. Forty dollars

I'll never pay back.

Angie moves on to her next victim and I settle in my seat, preparing to zone out. Especially when the talk turns to ideas on how to rekindle your marriage. My marriage burned out long ago, along with any desire to do anything about it. All Mark does is go to clubs and try to make a dollar with stupid jokes about his little wife and home life. All I do is tune him out, and go through my rotating list of who to siphon money from next. Not much relationship to work with.

Random bits of conversation stick with me. About little acts of attention, like cooking his favorite meal, and how to understand your man's feelings when he won't show them. Things like that. Things that make me laugh inside like Mark's jokes never do.

When we leave, Sandra pokes me in the side. "Have you been to one of Mark's performances lately? That would be like having lunch with him at work." She smiles. Sandra means well, and she mostly stays out of my business, so I don't mind her prodding this once.

I shrug. "I'm too busy keeping the lights on. And the gas." I pick at my chipped fingernails. "Think you could spot me forty?"

Sandra sighs, but keeps her smile. "Give it a try. He's yours, for better or worse."

I can't think of anything worse than going to one of Mark's gigs, but I nod and accept the two twenties. "I'll think about it."

I didn't think about it. Not really. But I didn't want to spend another evening alone in our shack. So I ask Sandra to drop me at the curb, two blocks from where Mark will do his thing about ten minutes from now. I don't tell her where I'm going, but Sandra's smarter than me. She gives me that knowing smile of encouragement before driving away.

I shuffle into the smoky bar. Mark is by the stage, talking with the animated owner. Mark's face is red with…what? Fear? Embarrassment? The owner isn't showering him with compliments.

Minutes later, Mark takes the stage. I stay back behind the pool tables, just out of his sight, and listen to each joke fall on deaf ears. No one cares he's up there, trying to entertain them. No one laughs. No one even knows he exists.

He looks desperate. As desperate as I feel. Our relationship is as flat as Mark's jokes.

Suddenly, I realize there is one person who cares, who knows Mark exists. One person who suddenly wants to take to heart the things she learned at that Bible thingy.

Me.

When booing brings Mark's show to a pitiful halt, he leaves the stage and heads for the side exit. I follow, catching the door before it swishes closed.

"Mark."

He spins as if shocked someone knows his name. I swallow a strange lump of pride I feel for my man, and hook my arm around his. He says, "I won't get paid tonight."

I squeeze his arm tighter and remember something from the Bible thingy. "How would you like homemade meatloaf like your mama used to make?"

Mark stares at me like I've lost my marbles. I give him a push toward our old junker in the parking lot. "But you gotta promise you won't turn it into one of your jokes if it tastes bad."

There isn't any laughter on the outside, but we both feel it inside. Mark tucks me closer to him and leads the way.

It Could Happen

Today, I'm not one of the fast drivers.

A certain comfort fills me as the clicking sound and flashing light of my blinker eases me into the right hand lane. Cruise set for the thirty mile drive to my hometown, I start thinking about the pages of the manuscript I began editing today.

Show the action. Add some dialogue. My red pen was hard at work until I reached the climax of the short story. That's when I called the writer.

"Hi Jill, it's Terri. Listen, I was just curious if this is based a true story."

"Uh, well, no, but it could happen. I mean, I think it's pretty realistic."

Indeed.

I hadn't been able to finish it. Not that I ran out of time.

When my coworkers laughed on their way out the front door of the publishing house, I realized I had been staring at the hummingbirds outside my three-by-three window. I had no idea how much time passed since I read the last sentence. I couldn't finish editing. Not today.

Like the stripes separating my car from collision with the eighteen-wheeler rocking past me, memory of the final paragraph flashes through my mind.

Abigail waved off the supporting hand and peered over the edge. Her hand shook as she ran it along the side of her head, feeling the warmth of her own blood. She stared in shock at the flame-engulfed car at the bottom of the ravine.

She screamed. "What have I done!"

I take the exit before my usual one. With speed at five miles an hour under the limit, I navigate the turns as if I travel this way often. Truth told, I had forgotten. Forgotten the pain, the fear, the confusion. Well, not forgotten. I chose not to remember. Until today.

Right signal activated, I turn into the Rose Hill Cemetery, an odd quiver upsetting my stomach. I make the half circle and ease my sedan to the curb.

"It could happen."

Jill's words accompany me as I walk through the lush grass, careful to step between the headstones. I kneel beside the grave, inhaling warm air filled with fragrances of spring. Dirt and fifteen years of grass cover the hole that had once haunted my nights.

Pieces of my client's story blend with my own memories.

Abigail couldn't believe she was stuck behind another slow car. Why couldn't people just drive the speed limit on two lane highways?

The yellow sign glared at her. "Sharp Curves Ahead. No Passing."

"Whatever." Good thing her mother wasn't in the car to lecture her. *"I've passed on this road before. Right up here, in fact. Looks clear…"*

The Honda roared when Abigail mashed the pedal to the floorboard. She checked the slow car as she glided by. A white haired head turned and wide eyes stared back at her.

Face forward again, the steering wheel slipped and Abigail lost control in the steepness of the curve. A clang of metal resounded as her car slammed into the other. She stomped on the brake and her car skidded sideways. Fast. Too fast. Rubber burned, and the car shook before the backend banged to a stop against the guardrail.

Stunned, Abigail struggled out of her car, keenly aware she had neglected her seatbelt. Again.

A van pulled over a dozen yards in front of her and the driver rushed to the broken guardrail. Abigail stumbled to it, gasping for air.

The man turned to her. "Are you all right?"

Abigail waved off the supporting hand and peered over the edge…

My breathing is labored. I shake my head as I trace the letters on the headstone: Danielle Knight. 1973-1995.

My best friend. She was young —and fast.

Crossed double yellow lines…excessive speed…lost control on curve…four dead… That's how our hometown paper reported it.

Pain fills my chest as I recall Jill's short story. Why write something like that? It's so sad.

"But it could happen." It could, Jill. It did.

And it could again.

"Yes, Lord. It could again. But maybe Jill's story will stop some, even one. God, help us get it to the ones who will listen." Lifting my eyes to the heavens, healing peace washes over me.

Back in my car, I navigate traffic, cars zooming past me.

Today, I'm not one of the fast drivers.

The Greatest Moment

Why did the sun not rise?

Darkness closed in on Mary as she stared into the starless sky. Would the darkness come to her soul again, this time consuming the very air she breathed?

She could no longer wait for the sun's light. Small clay jars in hand, she stepped from the house and started down the road. Quiet footsteps followed her. The fact she was not alone in her world of grief comforted her.

The sun still refused to show itself. Mary strained to make out the form of the tomb. The pound of her heart overlaid the soft exclamations of the other women. The stone was moved, the black entrance gaping at them. Mary touched the cold rock, and her eyes moved from the stone, taller than she, to the dark opening.

The first ray of the sun penetrated the gloomy interior. Mary gasped when the light revealed the vacant room.

Her spice jars slipped from her grasp and crashed on the

rocks. She jerked back and fled. There was only one place she could go, one thing she could do.

Back at the house, she cried, "Peter! John! You must come quickly. They have taken away the Lord from the tomb. We do not know where they have taken Him!" Mary tried to catch her breath. The two disciples ran past her down the road, their sandaled feet sending pebbles flying.

Hand pressed to her heart, Mary followed. She exchanged pained glances with the sobbing women as they passed her going back to the house.

Mary stumbled on the loose rocks and plunged forward. Groaning, she lifted her face to the rising sun.

"Why?" Her hands reached to cover her burning heart. "Was my grief not enough? Must I be separated from my Lord forever?"

The sound of footsteps brought Mary's focus back to the road in front of her. Simon Peter met her eyes, the unspoken question hanging between them. He gave a troubled shake of his head. Shoulders hunched, he continued back to the house.

Mary's feet refused to move. How could she go back without knowing? Yet where could she go for answers?

"Mary."

Something in John's eyes, in his voice, caused Mary's pulse to quicken. Studying his countenance, Mary knew he had seen something. Did he know where they had taken the Lord?

John said nothing more. He continued on the path behind Simon Peter.

Agony fresh, Mary turned her sandaled feet toward the tomb again. She would not—could not—leave until she knew where her precious Lord was.

Despite the sun's warmth on her back, chills coursed through Mary's body. Her palm rested against the stone that had sealed the tomb. Another sob rocked her body as she dipped her head to gaze inside.

"Woman, why are you weeping?"

Mary brushed away the tears to stare at the man whose floating voice had spoken the question. He sat at the head of the shelf where her Lord had lain.

Choking on the lump in her throat, Mary struggled with her answer. How could she explain to this stranger how her Lord had rescued her from the dark pit of demon possession and brought her into the light of His love? How could her anguish be summed in mere words?

"They have taken away my Lord and I do not know where they have laid Him." What more could she say? Mary struggled to breathe around the sobs that overcame her.

Unable to bear the emptiness of the tomb, Mary turned to let the sun touch her face. But the Gardener who stood in her path blocked the soothing rays from her.

"Woman, why are you weeping?"

Had she not just answered this question? How long would she be tormented?

"Please, sir, if You have carried Him away, tell me where You have laid Him and I will take Him away."

Her heart weighted beyond endurance, Mary longed for the warmth of the risen sun.

"Mary!"

The voice was unmistakable. Mary's head lightened and her heart exploded with joy. Her tears took on new meaning. Her vision cleared as she gazed upon the face outlined by the beams of sunlight. Eternal light flooded her soul. There was only one word she could breathe.

"Rabboni!"

The darkness was no more.

Third Side of the Coin

"How's our top story coming, Ace?" Mr. Jenson's nickname for her had a flattering ring to it—three months ago. Now it was pure mockery. Amanda closed her laptop with a snap before he saw the screen, and rocked back in her thirteen-hour office chair, cigarette pack in hand.

"Fine, Chief. Just fine."

His breath touched her neck, blowing strands of bleached blonde hair as he leaned over her shoulder.

"Better have it wrapped up by Monday, Ace, or we'll change your name to something more akin to Mud."

Amanda tapped a cigarette out of the pack like his threat didn't affect her in the least. She waited until he turned away before lighting it. Her hand shook.

"Monday." Jenson moved past her and disappeared into his office, the gold lettering stating *Ray Jenson, Editor-in-Chief.*

Amanda flicked her lighter and inhaled, drawing the cigarette to life. What she really needed was a drink. She checked her silver-faced wristwatch, a coveted Christmas bonus from the newspaper two years ago. Now it was a constant reminder of her faltering investigative reporter career. But it still gave the accurate time of twelve-thirty. A long afternoon ahead, especially if her source didn't call. Again.

She stood, removed the cigarette and faced the desk behind her. "Hey, Nichols, how about some lunch?"

Tom Nichols rearranged the sticky notes plastered all over his desk, never lifting his eyes to her. "Uh, actually, I ate. I mean, I'm having lunch. I have plans."

Amanda snorted and stripped her jacket from the back of her chair. "Sure."

There was a time when rookie reporters tripped over themselves at a chance to have lunch with her. There was a time she wouldn't dream of asking them. Times change.

At her favorite eatery, nothing on the menu appealed to her. But she'd lost six pounds with her tanked appetite, so why complain?

~~~

There was no point in returning to the newspaper office. Jenson might jump her again about the story she'd touted as a month's worth of front page material.

After driving the back streets in a fruitless search for her key contact, Amanda pulled her pearl white Lexus into the drive of her two-story lakefront home. While waiting for the garage door to open, she shook her head at the showy sight. How stupid for someone who lived alone to own such a place. Her brains had taken a vacation when she received her inheritance from her parents' estate. But then, no one advertised her as being smart.

The red light on the answering machine blinked when she tossed her keys in the tray next to it. For a delirious moment hope rushed in. Maybe Bonners left a message…

Get a grip, Ace. He doesn't have your stupid unlisted number. Amanda frowned as she punched the play button with a thin finger. She stepped around the granite island to the glossy oak cabinets in her too-large kitchen. Her hand enclosed the friendly glass tumbler as the message began to play.

"Hey Sis, couldn't get you on your cell. Just thought I'd see what you're up to this weekend. Friend of mine got extra tickets to the game. Thought you might wanna go. Give me a call."

Good thing Ryan's message was short. Amanda always tingled with guilt if she deleted it before his good-bye. Now a zero showed in the number slot for messages. Amanda turned to her liquor cabinet. It was stupid to start drinking this early in the day, but she relished the freedom that came with no one around to say she couldn't.

~~~

Monday dawned and Amanda unlocked the office for the first time in months. With her early arrival surprise, she had a better chance of pulling off her con. She could fool Jenson as long as she managed to come across as confident as she had been a year ago. That would impress him more than anything.

Nichols arrived minutes later. Amanda, settled in her leather mahogany rolling chair, swiveled around and practiced her catty smile on him. "Morning, Nichols. Throw a dog a bone?"

The younger man smiled as he placed his laptop bag in his desk chair. "Doesn't look like you need one. Finally get a break in your story?"

Amanda's face heated at the condescension in his voice. "Maybe. You know, I was reading one of your lame adverb riddled articles. How do you keep a job?"

He cocked an eyebrow and she swore he hid a smile. Okay, so it wasn't the greatest comeback, but it warmed her up for the big man. She should've listened to her gut last night though, and cut the drinking while she worked on the story. And her plan to pitch it.

Jenson walked in and headed for his office. Amanda spun back to face her desk, spine straight, watching the boss from the corner of her eye. He didn't glance her way. Not a good start. But she had to do it now before she chickened out— another term for *career over*.

She entered Jenson's office without a knock and strode toward him, her trademark smile pasted carefully in place. He sat behind his desk, eyes glued on his computer screen, cigarette barely hanging between his lips. Classic picture of an old time newspaper editor, sans the typewriter. She dropped her printout in the center of his paper chaos.

"Hope you like it." Amanda did a smooth one-eighty and walked out, not glancing back. Before the office door drifted closed, Jenson screeched. Nichols looked up from his sticky notes.

Amanda mimicked his cocked eyebrow. "That's how it's done, kid." Hand on the arm of her chair, she made a show to drop in it when Jenson's voice boomed through the now full office.

"Sinclair, get in here!"

Her smug expression directed at Nichols helped her keep a grip on her composure. Showtime.

Jenson closed the door after she reentered the office, and he pointed to the leather chair in front of his desk.

"Sit."

Amanda folded her arms. She couldn't stop the tremble in her hands. Not even mid-morning and it was worse than ever.

"That's okay, Chief. I'll stand."

Jenson paused as he rounded his desk. His right hand clutched her article. He held it up. "Where did you get this?"

Heart pounding an offbeat tune, Amanda concentrated on her practiced, but dazzling, performance. "I have my sources. Four weeks ago, my top guy saw Mayor Harper checking into a hotel in the slums. He didn't report anything else, so I put my dogs on it. They turned up all the evidence listed in the article, proving our quaint little straight-laced conservative mayor is indeed having an affair with the esteemed Council-woman Banks." *Almost all the evidence. It was only that little bit I added until I hear confirmation from Bonners.* "Remember, she and her husband separated about that time."

Jenson scanned the article as she spoke. Amanda stepped to his desk and bumped a cigarette from his pack. She positioned herself to prevent him from catching the tremble if he happened to look up. Sheer confidence coated her exterior. Inside, she crumpled.

"This is brilliant," Jenson murmured as he moved to sit on the edge of his desk near Amanda. "Simply brilliant. No one else is on to this, not even a whisper."

"The mayor is a careful man."

Jenson glanced up with the half grin Amanda craved to see again. "Front page if I ever published one. Good job, Ace."

Amanda managed to keep all her air from gushing out. She pointed her chin at her boss. "Anytime, Chief."

She took the rest of the day off, not relishing the moment when the special edition hit the stands that evening. She wanted to hide out until the media storm ended.

~~~

Her cell rang at 3:00 a.m..

The number looked vaguely familiar, but in her condition she couldn't give her own full name. Amanda mumbled into the mouthpiece.

"What?"

The male voice swore. "What were you thinking, writing that story? If there's a slander lawsuit, my name'd better not come up."

"Sure, Bonners. Whatever."

"Whatever's right. You're wrong, all wrong. The mayor wasn't having an affair—I know the whole story now."

Amanda tried to sit up, knocking her empty glass tumbler off the nightstand as she fumbled for the lamp switch. "What are you talking about? You said—"

"*You* didn't give me a chance to find the truth. This is major league stuff. Front page for a month. Harper and Banks were meeting in secret while they worked on exposing corruption in the criminal courts. They were set to blow five upstanding judges outta the water. But you couldn't wait. All you wanted to do was drag a clean politician's name through the mud to save your lousy career. Like I said, you rat on me and I'll turn over every dirty rock I have on you. That's no bluff. Oh, and get yourself a new birddog."

"Bonners? Bonners!" Amanda pulled the phone away from her ear and checked. Call ended. Her stomach lurched but there was nothing to throw up but alcohol. And nothing left to do but wait for the rocks to rain down.

~~~

The next morning Amanda didn't answer Jenson's first three calls. She expected him to at least leave messages, ranting a blue streak. He didn't. She answered the fourth call.

"You're fired."

"Look, Mr. Jenson, I can explain—"

"Shut up, *Ace*." There was a razor edge in his voice. Or maybe it was the vodka Amanda had been swigging all morning. Whichever, she knew something more had happened as her boss continued. "Can't you even remember why Mrs. Banks separated from her husband? You broke the story."

"What about it?" Amanda struggled to put force in her voice but it still sounded mousy.

"Her husband was a mental case. She was trying to get him help."

"*Was?*"

"He's dead. So's she. So's the mayor. After reading the story, wacky husband killed them both before turning the gun on himself. Hope you're proud of your work. The police will have some questions for you. I told them everything."

It was Amanda who ended this call. The home phone rang. So much for an unlisted number. Someone at the newspaper probably leaked it.

Then the truth whacked her with such force her knees buckled and she hit the floor. They were dead? It couldn't be…

The doorbell rang. The answering machine clicked on. Amanda slid flat on her back as her cell went off. She threw it at the wall and the sound stopped.

Her mind buzzed with the desperate wish she could stop time—and reverse it.

~~~

Amanda plopped down at her kitchen table with the full glass tumbler in hand. The sound of the ice clinking against it was a relief compared to the constant ring of the phone and doorbell. She ignored the burn as the alcohol slid down her throat. It better do its job.

A click at the back door announced someone had turned a key in the lock. She didn't bother checking, and poured the glass full to the rim as Ryan's face came into view. He pulled out a chair on the other side of the kitchen table and turned it around, straddling it as he crossed his arms on the wood back. The smell of his cologne and her alcohol made a sickly sweet combination.

Front teeth showed with his boyish smile. "You look terrible."

"Thanks, little brother. You can leave now."

"Tough day?"

The phone rang with vengeance. Amanda smirked. "Lesson learned. Make one bad call and your whole life gets sucked down the tubes."

"Only one bad call?"

Amanda set her jaw. "I should've known you just came to preach at me. You always—"

"I'm not preaching, Sis. I want to see you get your life back together—"

Amanda rose to a crouching position and raked her arm across the table, sending the glass tumbler to the floor with a crash.

"You know nothing about my life! You have no idea what I've done." A sob choked her words as she dropped back into the chair. "Don't say God will forgive me. Don't say you'll forgive me. Three people are dead. *Dead.* And none of it was even true."

"So you did fabricate the whole story."

"No—not at first." Amanda laid her forehead on the edge of the table and rubbed a fist across her throbbing eyes. She had to pull herself together.

She stiffened her back, which felt like a rotted board, and grabbed the pack of cigarettes. She pulled one out, placed it between her lips, but when she tried to ignite the lighter her fingers refused to cooperate. Ryan took it, flicked once and held the flame to the tip.

Amanda puffed and sputtered. "Look, I thought I was really on to something. Had reliable sources, convincing circumstantial evidence. I told the editor I needed a little more time to confirm. He said I'd better have it wrapped up by Monday. I didn't. I told him I did. He trusted me, ran it front page. Now three people are dead and I find out I was wrong. Career finished. Criminal charges looming. End of my story."

Amanda took a few drags before mashing the half-burnt butt in her ashtray. She pulled out another one and twirled it in her fingertips. "Well? Isn't this the part where you say I'm going to hell?"

Ryan stared at the smoke drifting from the ashtray. He reached in his jean pocket and held a quarter out in her view.

"Ever heard the story about the third side of the coin?"

"Believe me, I am not in the mood for stories." Amanda stood and wobbled to the glossy oak cabinet, pulling down another glass tumbler. Where had her first one disappeared to? Ryan's gaze tickled her neck hairs.

When she returned to her seat, he continued. "One side is heads, the other tails. But what about the third side?"

He stood the quarter on its end and flicked it, sending the coin spinning across the table. Amanda slapped it flat, her anger breeding impatience. "What third side?"

"The third side is the one that holds the other two together. The edge. It's the connection between them. We're like heads and tails, Sis. The third side is understanding. The love of family. The love God has for us. Look at it. It's a continuous circle."

Amanda uncovered the quarter. She flipped it into her palm.

Ryan put his hand over it. "Unending understanding. Unending love."

Amanda let her hand dangle when Ryan removed his. Somewhere through the years, her little brother's Christian faith had given him something she couldn't comprehend. She stared at the coin.

"I'll swing by later with some dinner. Pizza still your favorite comfort food?"

She lifted her gaze to see the boyish smile and nodded. "Yeah."

"I'll pick one up. We can hang out for a bit."

"Okay." Amanda swallowed and stuck the cigarette between her lips. "Thanks."

She ran her thumb around the edge of the coin. Strange comfort to know she would never reach the end of it.

Return…to your family, and

I will deal well with you. Gen 32:9

That's What
Family Is For

Blackie

"Finish up kids, we'll be late."

Hannah shoved the last chunk of jelly-filled donut in her mouth, elbows on the table, eyes never leaving her daddy's face. She chewed and swallowed. "It's only nine-thirty, Daddy. Church starts at ten. We have lots of time."

"We can't be late. I promised Mom…"

Hannah stiffened when her daddy, Paul, frowned. But he wasn't angry, at least not with her or Charlie.

Paul wadded the empty pastry papers together. "Wipe your mouths and meet me at the door." He stumbled over his feet as he hurried to the waste bin of the small downtown pastry shop.

"Why we go to church?" Charlie sucked the donut glaze from one finger at a time. "Daddy don't like it no more."

Hannah picked up a leftover napkin and wiped the corners of Charlie's mouth. "Before the angels took her to Heaven,

Daddy promised Mommy that we would go to church. Daddy always keeps his promises."

"Let's go." Paul propped the door open with his back, hands buried in his coat.

Next to their car, Hannah held Charlie's hand while Paul rummaged through his pockets. Tiny beads of sweat dotted his forehead despite the cold February wind.

"Daddy, how come the keys in the seat?" Charlie's question brought the world to a halt.

"Oh no." Paul cupped his hands on the tinted passenger window, peering inside. "And it's Sunday. It'll take hours for a locksmith. No, God, we can't be late."

Hannah's eyes flooded with tears. *I wish Mommy were here.*

"I use'ta have a black coat like that."

Hannah's eyes widened at the stranger hunkered over a rusty shopping cart. He wore a funny-looking hat and gloves but his bare fingers showed. Hannah put a finger under her nose, wishing the man wasn't standing so close.

"Yes sir, I use'ta love everything black—black shoes, black suits, even my truck was black. Drove my Lucy crazy."

Hannah glanced up. Her daddy rolled his eyes as he pulled out his cell phone. Before he touched the keypad, the man spoke again.

"Name's Blackie and I can get that door open without a scratch. Ain't nobody gonna get here anytime soon."

Not waiting for a reply, the man pulled an odd-looking device from his shopping cart. "Won't take but a minute."

Paul frowned. "Hey, wait a—"

"Don't wanna be late, do ya?"

Hannah saw a flicker of pain in her daddy's eyes. That held him in place long enough for Blackie to open the passenger side door with ease.

"There ya go." Blackie replaced his magical tool under a pile of newspapers in his cart.

The family didn't move until Blackie began wheeling his cart away. "Wait!" Paul slid his wallet out and offered the man a twenty-dollar bill. "Here."

Blackie looked at him, his eyes twinkling like her daddy's had not so long ago.

"Just put it in the offerin' plate at church, brother. We'll say it's my tithe for the week."

Paul slowly replaced the twenty and reached to shake Blackie's hand. "Thanks. I don't know why, but I believe we were supposed to meet today." Paul took off his coat and draped it around Blackie's shoulders.

Blackie just nodded and started walking, his cart creaking like fingernails dragging across a blackboard.

Hannah stepped to her daddy's side, slipping her hand in his. "We need to go, Daddy. We'll be late."

Paul watched the man disappear around the corner, then squatted eye level with Hannah and placed his cold hands on her cheeks. "I think it'll be okay, sweetie. Mommy will understand."

Hannah's lips quivered. It was the first time since Mommy went to Heaven that her daddy had spoken directly to her. The hollow look in his eyes had vanished and in its place was a faint twinkle.

Colors

Wayne entered the kitchen, immediately noting his sister's *boy-I'm-mad-at-the-world look*. He lowered his brief bag against the wall and set a load of groceries on the kitchen counter. "Hey Sis, how'd it go today?"

Liz rustled the plastic grocery bags, retrieving two cans. "Well, I picked Sammy up from the slumber party around eleven. I thought she had a good time, until we got in the car." She walked to the pantry and continued in her edged tone. "On the way home, she started crying and saying 'She's mean!' When we got home, she didn't want to talk, play games, *nothing*." Liz tossed her hands and let them slap her jeans. "Really, I don't know why kids have to be so cruel."

Wayne's gut had told him Sammy wasn't ready to go places without him. Eight was a tough age for any girl, but Sammy…

His arm rested across Liz's shoulders. "She's in her room?"

"Yeah. I'll put up the groceries, then I'm meeting Mom at

the church. We need to finish VBS decorating." Liz returned his hug.

"Thanks, tell Mom I said hi."

In the privacy of the hallway, Wayne rested his forehead against the door and listened to the muffled crying on the other side. *Lord, help me help her.* Wayne didn't expect an instant reply. It never happened that way.

He opened the door to find Sammy sitting cross-legged on her bed in the midst of her stuffed gorillas. Her favorite, Samson, was tucked under her chin, tears soaking into his fur. Wayne stepped toward her. "Hey, what's the matter with my princess?"

Eyes squeezed shut, Sammy coughed out the words. "She's mean, Daddy! She's so mean."

Wayne sat on the edge of the bed behind Sammy. She fell back and he caught her shaking frame on his chest. He stroked his little girl's hair, memories of his own mother's comfort touching him. He wanted her wisdom. His own well of encouraging words was running dry. "It's okay. Tell me what happened. Who was being mean?"

"Janet."

Wayne sighed to himself as he looked toward the wall for a second. "How was she mean this time?"

"Right in front of everybody, she asked, 'What's *your* favorite color, Sammy?' She's the meanest kid in the world!"

Sammy's tears began again. Wayne pulled her onto his lap and rocked her back and forth.

Her tears slowly subsided.

"Daddy, what are colors really like?"

The question caught Wayne off guard for a moment, but he smiled at the images coming to mind. God provided.

"Let's go to the backyard."

Fingers intertwined, Wayne walked with Sammy, allowing her to lead the way. Sammy moved with confidence in her familiar surroundings.

As they stepped onto the back deck, Wayne paused. Sammy stopped. "What, Daddy?"

"Stand here a minute. What do you feel?"

"A little funny, just standing here." Wisps of Sammy's hair blew into her face. She brushed them aside.

"Colors aren't just something you see, you can feel them. The sun is yellow, but how does it feel? Warm, comforting? Close your eyes and turn your face to the sun. What do you feel?"

"I don't know."

"Come on. Just try."

Sammy turned her face to the sky, the sun's full rays reflecting on her smooth complexion. "Happy, I guess. Like I wanna smile."

Wayne didn't hold back his own smile. "Yeah, happy. Yellow's a happy color. When you wonder what it looks like, just think of how good the sun makes you feel. That's yellow."

"Okay." Sammy dropped her chin to her chest, bottom lip puckered. Wayne knew she was trying to process the information around the hurt in her heart.

"Let's do a different color." A quick squeeze of hands brought Sammy along as Wayne stepped forward. "The tire swing."

Sammy didn't miss a beat as she strode to the end of the porch and down the two steps to the grassy yard. If only she carried that confidence everywhere. *In time*, Wayne promised.

When they reached the tire swing hanging from the ancient oak tree, Sammy climbed in and Wayne gave a shove on the cool rubber. "Remember the stories I've told you about me and Uncle Robby?"

"About how you used to play on a tire swing like this?"

"My big brother looked after me when we were kids. Then he grew up and protected us when he joined the military. He was wounded in battle, so our country gave him the Purple Heart. Purple's a color of courage and bravery."

"So when I think of Uncle Robby, I'll know how the color purple feels."

The tension exited Wayne's chest. How fast his baby learned. "Remember when you asked Jesus into your heart?"

Sammy held on to the inside rim of the tire and leaned back as the swing lazily circled above the ground. She smiled. "I felt clean on the inside."

"When we repent and accept Christ as our Savior, He washes us white as snow."

"White's awesome."

"One of my favorite colors."

"Mine too."

Wayne glanced around, searching for another color. The warm sun, the creak of the tire swing in the breeze, the coolness of the grass beneath his bare feet…wait, his feet weren't bare. "Take off your shoes."

"Are you going to?"

Work boots and socks tossed aside, Wayne sat cross-legged in the grass. "Can't you smell my feet?"

Sammy giggled and climbed out of the tire swing. She kicked off her flip flops and plopped beside him.

"Tear off a blade of grass. It's green and green covers most of God's creation. How does it feel when you walk through the grass barefoot?"

"Good. Fun." Sammy giggled as she shredded the blade. "The grass tickles my feet."

"Let's lay in it." Wayne propped his head with one hand as he lay on his side, watching Sammy roll to her back. His baby girl. Only eight years old with a patchwork of life comprehended, yet so much to learn. Wayne ran his free hand through Sammy's golden brown hair, spreading it around her head. "Let's feel the color orange. God puts out orange at fall time. There's the big round pumpkins you love. The leaves change from green to bright yellows, reds, and oranges—"

"Orange makes me feel close to family."

Wayne cocked his head. Sammy's eyes were drifting closed. "Why's that?"

"Because of Thanksgiving. The world is full of orange and that's when we all get together. It feels so snuggly."

"I guess orange is like our family color."

Sammy's eyes closed. She breathed a heavy sigh and rolled to her side away from Wayne. "What about red? Janet says she looks so pretty in red."

Wayne shut his eyes, images of red dancing in his thoughts, but he didn't feel anything. He opened his eyes and stared at the tangle of his little girl's hair. The feeling overwhelmed him. "Well, baby girl, red's a beautiful color to see. But that's nothing compared to how it makes me feel." He sat up halfway and drew the small frame of his little girl to his beating heart. "The first time I held you, I understood the color red. Red is love. And that was a kind of love I never knew before."

Sammy pulled away and turned to face Wayne, her sightless eyes spilling tears. "Next time Janet asks what my favorite color is, I'll know what to say. Red, because it makes me feel just how much my daddy loves me."

Head-Locked

In all my eight years, I couldn't remember a single time I admired my brother. Maybe because he was always getting *me* in trouble when *he* did something wrong.

But I was set to have fun on our family's summer vacation in Branson, Missouri. Nothing could dampen my enthusiasm as we traveled down the stairs in the Cathedral Room for a tour of Silver Dollar City's Marvel Cave. The whole place smelled like cold and wet mixed together.

"Wow! Look how far down that is!" Keeping one hand on the guardrail, I caught my dad's sleeve and tugged. "Are we going to see any bats?"

"We might, Son. You just remember to follow the rules we discussed."

"Yes, sir." I gazed at the ceiling two hundred feet above. "Wow! Can you imagine falling from there?"

My parents were a half flight of stairs below when Tommy

grabbed the back of my shirt. "If you say 'wow' one more time, I'm gonna put you in a head-lock."

I gulped and caught up with the group.

"In 1869, explorers entered the cave searching for minerals," the tour guide was saying. "As it turned out, the only thing ever mined here was bat guano."

"Bats?" My six-year-old sister turned bug-eyed. Tommy wasn't going to miss this opportunity. With the feather he'd collected earlier, he brushed the back of Janie's neck, sending her flying to our mother. "Mommy, a bat got me!"

I wondered why my dad was staring at me—until I saw my brother's angelic face with a finger pointing my direction.

"Since you can't keep your hands to yourself, Matthew," Dad said, "You will hold your mother's for awhile."

The dreaded punishment! Not that I minded holding my mom's hand…but to be forced like a toddler was beyond embarrassing.

I trudged through the Shoe Room, not caring about the giant footprint in the ceiling. At Dad's nod, my mother released my hand with a squeeze and a soft warning. "Behave."

Soon the narrow corridors, lit by a string of bare bulbs, had my mouth gapping again. "Wow," I said in a voice Tommy couldn't hear, "This is so cool."

Entering another room, I trotted to a rail on the left and gazed at the slanted wall beyond. It vanished in blackness. "Wonder what's up there?" A tingle of excitement rushed through me as I imagined exploring the cave on my own. Just like Huckleberry—

"Psst!"

I jumped when Tommy grabbed my shoulders from behind. "Why don't we see where that goes?"

I gulped. There would be no mild punishment if we were

caught. I glanced at the group climbing up the far stairs. Our parents probably thought we were behind them.

"It'll only take a couple of minutes." Before I could reply, Tommy scooped me up and set me over the guardrail.

Tommy had straddled the pipe rail when a deep voice froze us. "What do you think you're doing?" Our father was striding across the rocky floor to us. Tommy looked down at me, on the wrong side of the fence.

Uh-oh.

My brother scrambled off the rail while my father lifted and set me in front of him on shaky legs. "Matthew, I warned you..."

"It was my fault, Dad. I made him do it."

My jaw dropped as I stared at my big brother. His eyes met our father's.

Dad was caught off guard, but quickly recovered. "You and I will address this tonight—privately." We all knew what "address" meant.

Climbing the stairs past the rushing waterfall, my brother and I were kept between our parents. I spoke to Tommy in a masked voice. "You really told Dad it was your fault!"

"Don't make a big deal outta it."

The group paused to take pictures of the falls. "But why didn't you tell him it was my fault?"

"It wasn't."

"But—"

"Look." Tommy put his nose to mine. "Don't you go repeating this." He frowned, then sighed. "I was remembering about Paul and how his little brother was almost run over by a car 'cause he was following Paul to our house on his bike. Everybody was really mad and Paul got in trouble. That's when I got to thinking maybe I *should* be looking after my little brother. You know, like Dad says, start growing up and being a godly man."

I could only shake my head. "Wow."

For the first time in my life, I actually admired my brother. Even if he did put me in a head-lock right then and there.

Mommy Always
Cuts My Hair

Aunt Julie pulled the comforter to my chin, and messed up my hair. "Tomorrow will be time for a trip to the barbershop, Little Man."

The jitters in my tummy jumped to my lips. "Those big chairs scare me. Can't Mommy come back for a little bit? Just to cut my hair?"

My jitters went to Aunt Julie's lips, but she didn't sound scared—much—when she said, "There's nothing to be afraid of, Jimmy. The people at the barbershop are nice."

"But I don't wanna. Please, can't Mommy do it one more time? Please?"

"It won't hurt. I promise."

"You said that Jesus loves me, and that Mommy and Daddy are with Him because the car got messed up and they're in Heaven. If they all love me, won't Jesus let Mommy come back for a little while to cut my hair? Please?"

Aunt Julie didn't say anything. She turned off my Tigger lamp, and went to the bedroom door. The bright light from the hallway sparkled on the wetness of her face.

Why did my talking always make her cry? Mommy wouldn't like it if I was making Aunt Julie cry. I would just have to stop talking to her.

~~~

I swung my legs faster, wishing my feet could touch the black and white checkerboard floor of the barbershop. I stared at the big chairs where people sat getting their hair cut. My feet would *never* touch the floor from there.

Aunt Julie tugged on my hand. "It won't take but a few minutes."

The walk across the checkerboard floor took forever as I shuffled my feet. Everything smelled like wet hair.

The man holding a pair of scissors looked like a giant—even beside that gigantic chair. "Hello there, son. Ready for a cut?"

My feet came off the floor. I was covered all over with a black plastic blanket. Aunt Julie touched my nose with a cold finger. "I'll be sitting right over there, okay?"

I shook my head for yes. I hadn't talked to Aunt Julie all morning, but she had still cried when we left the house.

After whispering a long time to the barbershop man, she went way off by the big windows where we'd been first.

I wondered if the man knew about the butterflies in my tummy. "Well, Jimmy, your aunt tells me this is your first trip to the barber's chair." He picked up a spray bottle. "You must be a big boy. How old are you?" When he squirted my hair, the tickle of water on my scalp almost made me giggle. Almost.

I tried to hold out my fingers, but he couldn't see them through the black blanket. I looked up at him. "Six."

"I tell you what the trick is to having a conversation while getting your hair cut." The chair swiveled. I tried to grab for something so I wouldn't fall.

"See that big mirror? Keep your eyes on it. That way we can talk without you moving your head. Okay?"

I shook my head for yes. Wait, I wasn't supposed to do that. I looked in the mirror. The man looked back at me. He was smiling.

"You can call me Mark."

"Yes, sir."

Mr. Mark moved to the other side of me, squirting more water. "Talking's a good thing, Jimmy. Helps you figure out things you don't understand." He picked up the scissors and I watched him work in the mirror.

"Yes, sir."

"Do you like talking with your Aunt Julie?"

I started to shake my head again, but stopped. "I always make her sad when I ask her something."

Mr. Mark paused and looked at me in the mirror. "What things make her sad?"

"When I ask about Mommy and Daddy and why they can't come home."

"Do you know why they can't come home?"

The shake made it halfway this time. "'Cause they're in Heaven with Jesus. But if Jesus loves us, why can't He let them come home sometimes? I want Mommy to cut my hair."

My neck hurt from keeping it so still as I watched Mr.

Mark. He stepped to a small table and picked up a shorter comb. "Sometimes it's hard to face things and talk about them." He combed my hair to one side, his scissors cutting chunks and sending them to the floor. "But you know, Aunt Julie would like to talk with you anyway. You'll understand the rest soon. Just always remember, no matter what, Jesus *does* love you."

I still didn't want to face Aunt Julie. But maybe…"Mr. Mark?"

From over my head, he looked at me in the mirror. "Yeah, Jimmy?"

"It's easier to talk to the mirror."

Mr. Mark smiled. "True, Jimmy. True."

That's when I decided to talk to Aunt Julie again. And I knew the right place for both of us—in the mirror.

Plastic Swords &
Book Reports

Meg squealed. "Grammy, Matt's aggravating me again!"

When Hope walked into the living room, Meg grabbed her hand. Matt's sigh was filled with frustration. "She won't play with me!"

Hope put a hand on each of her grandchildren. "You two need to learn to get along. All this fussing and fighting brings nothing but harm. Now, what's the problem?"

Meg opened her mouth, but Matt beat her to it. "She's been sitting in her chair all day reading and scribbling. I wanted her to play sword fight with me, but she just turned up her nose. There's no one else for me to play with, and she's being mean!"

"Am not!"

"Are too!"

"Am not—"

"Quiet." Hope sent up a prayer for wisdom. "All right, Meg, let's hear your side of it."

"I'm trying to finish reading this book so I can write a report on it. I—"

"A report?" Matt groaned. "School's out. You spend too much time reading and writing when we could be—"

"Matt." Hope managed to keep the edge from her voice. "Let Meg finish."

Matt pinned his lips together, legs spread and braced, clenching his plastic sword with both hands. He looked ready to use it.

Meg lifted her chin. "I want to write a report for Aunt Mary. She gave me the book and I want her to know how much I like it. But I can't get it done because Matt's been pestering me all day. All he ever wants to do is play, so he pokes me with that thing until I finally give in. But I don't want to play, I wanna read!"

Another prayer went up before Hope spoke. "It sounds like y'all need to find some common ground. Jesus said we should come and reason together. I think you two are old enough to do that on your own."

She dropped her hands from their shoulders. "Use the next hour to think of something you both enjoy. You'll spend the rest of the afternoon doing that. And if I don't hear any bickering, tomorrow you both can do what you like—separately, no bugging each other. Agreed?"

The two children puckered their lips at their grandmother. Meg spoke first. "There's nothing we both like to do."

"Pray about it and I know you'll think of something. You do have a whole hour." Without waiting for further protests, Hope went back in the kitchen. The smell of cookies baking should give her grandchildren extra incentive.

~~~

Less than the hour later, a squeal called Hope to the living room again.

"What is going on?" Hope's rebuke was sharper than she'd intended, but the sight of Matt thrusting his plastic sword at the paper waving Meg nearly undid her. Would these children ever listen to her?

Two pairs of chocolate brown eyes turned to meet Hope's. "We're playing, Grammy," came the unison reply. They giggled.

"Meg wrote a play about a big sword fight between a knight and a dragon," Matt said, a hint of pride in his voice. "And since I'm the sword fighting expert, I get to be the knight and she's the dragon. It's fun, especially 'cause I know how it ends."

Hope's shoulder muscles melted. "That sounds very good. How does it end?"

Meg chimed in. "It has a happy ending, Grammy. The knight and dragon figure out that if they work together instead of fighting, they can overthrow the queen of the kingdom."

An eyebrow shot up. "And who might the queen be?"

Two plastic swords turned on her.

Innocence
of the Innocent

A trip to the grocery store with her five-year-old son never ended without incident. Katherine had lived through it all: stomping feet past the candy aisle, and a "Can we go now?" whine to set a clock by. The infamous cry of "I need to go" three times in a half hour, and the scaling of a canned goods display. Yet nothing prepared Katherine for Andy's crowning moment. Or maybe it was hers.

On the trek down aisle three, they bumped into Jackie, an unmarried friend from church. Katherine grimaced but pasted a smile on her face. Why hadn't she started at the bottom of her grocery list?

She put a thick layer of syrup on each word. "Jackie, how are you?"

"I'm good, thanks. You?" Jackie hauled her loaded cart to

a stop and checked the status of her sleeping newborn.

"She's such a doll," Katherine cooed, glancing at the little angel tucked in her carrier.

Andy stood on tiptoe next to the cart. "I wanna see!"

Katherine lifted him to the best vantage point then lowered him back to his feet. Andy directed his question at Jackie. "Is that your baby?"

The woman chuckled. Andy's next words tumbled out. "Mommy told Daddy she wasn't sure whose baby it was."

Katherine would never again doubt the term *dead silence*. It filled the space between her and Jackie like liquid. No way to breathe. Bright red flooded over Katherine's cheeks and spread down her neck. How much easier it had been to re-stack the canned goods display.

Her mind replayed the conversation she'd had with her husband the night before. She'd just hung up the phone from talking with a close friend at church, who shared a fairly juicy bit about Jackie. Surely her low tone and the Veggie Tales movie was ample safety precaution against young ears.

But God heard it. Think before you speak, Katherine. How great a forest fire a little match can start…

Katherine tried to drain the liquid silence with a dumb response. "I don't know what to say."

Jackie laughed the only way she could—awkwardly. "It's okay. I gotta go. Bye."

~~~

Katherine didn't go to church for three straight Sundays. She spent that time studying Scripture and in deep prayer.

By the third Sunday she felt prepared to sit at the kitchen table and write a letter of apology to Jackie. The tone reflected her regret at speaking of something that was none of her business to begin with. She signed the letter with a sigh.

Andy galloped in. He leaned on Katherine's knee, and stuck a piece of paper in her face. "Look what we learned in Sunday School."

Katherine examined the scribbles with admiration. "Good job, Andy. What was the lesson about?"

"Mousetraps. They help us remember our tongues can say bad things and trap us and hurt other people too."

Katherine smiled. *Thank You, Lord. I think Andy and I need another trip to the grocery store to buy Mommy a mousetrap—and have a talk about repeating things we hear.*

Long & Short

He reached for another fistful of water and swung it in a half circle before releasing it behind as he gasped for air. In the same motion, he twisted and reached out his other hand to repeat the process.

"Go, Long! You are doing well!"

The cry of his sister in their native tongue pushed him to kick a little harder and grab a larger fistful of water as the black mark on the pool wall drew close. He brushed it with his fingertips and pulled his legs under himself to get a maximum push off the wall. Eleven laps to go.

Long still laughed inside himself about this moment. Here he was, at the finals. A world stage. The Olympic Games. Who would have dreamed that the one who finally represented their country at the Games would be a poor man's son?

After clumsy attempts at winter sports, Long finally dove in their icy pond and never stopped swimming. Only by chance did a foreigner see him one day. Or rather he spotted Long's sister, Short. The romance was brief. She laughed at the foreigner, but still convinced him to help Long achieve his lifelong dream of making the Olympics. A former champion swimmer, the man had all the connections and enough interest, at the time, to help. Short still laughed about the man. Long never knew his name.

His shoulders began their familiar burn, the point when he gained speed. He checked the time before brushing the wall. Record! A record loomed if he kept this pace.

He'd never swam in a pool before diving into the practice one three weeks ago. The sense of laughter shrouded him during attempts to master the wall turn. He had studied the others, but couldn't imitate their body movements.

The next turn loomed. Short had encouraged him to do what worked best for him, not everyone else. She helped him master his full thrust position that always sent him ahead of the field at the start. Time to use it after checking the board. He'd fallen off slightly.

Long took another quick breath, a grin on his face he hoped Short could see. She shouted encouragement again, just as she had standing on the banks of that icy pond.

When he received his country's support and the paperwork flooded in, Long noted Short's name listed as his spouse. In spite of their attempts to explain the situation, no one seemed competent enough to correct the error. So, Long and Short laughed all the way to the airport together.

The thought of Short's illness crowded his mind. Doctors said she wouldn't live much longer, but Long had made her promise that if he did well in his first Olympics, she would help him get to the next. She'd promised. Short never broke a promise to him.

At the next turn, he was a full second under the record.

Every kind of mistake had been made to bring them to this moment. The disqualified trio that allowed him in the semi-finals, and then the disqualifications that put him in the finals, giving him a chance to churn water with the best the world had to offer.

Blunders abounded on this journey. Two days ago, a fellow swimmer had given him a book. When Long cocked his head in question, the guy said in broken French, which Long could barely speak, "Didn't you say you wanted one?"

Long shook his head. The guy laughed and slapped his back. "Keep it anyway. I have more."

When Long gave the book to Short, who could read French, he chuckled but she was interested. He asked what it was, and she smiled, almost sadly. "It's a Bible."

Long had always feared the exposure Short had to the world at a young age. But something about her demeanor was peaceful. Perhaps another mistake for their good.

The final turn. He could hear Short's cheer, then all went silent. He glanced at the time. She would watch it, breathless as well. It was going to be close.

Every muscle in his body a sheer burning mass, Long extended his fingers and touched the wall, pulling up for air as he checked the time. A record. He had beaten his personal best.

A single clap sounded. He looked toward the lone observer who rose to her feet as she applauded. No matter the rest of the contestants had finished ten minutes ago. No matter no one else stayed to watch the end. All that mattered was his sister, his world stage. Her smile shined through her tears.

Long raised his arm in victory.

Grrr, Tiggers Don't Like Shuffleboard

It's not like we weren't close at one time. We were. My brother Tim and I did everything together. But I guess time changes things and sometimes when you grow up, you grow apart. At least that's the only thing I could figure. The good ol' days of childhood were a fumbled memory.

Awkwardness cloaked the day we spent together at our familiar stomping grounds, the resort that had become our second home so long ago.

"Wanna play some putt-putt?" I asked.

Tim shrugged. "Sure."

After two rounds in which my ball decided to go swimming each time, then being defeated in five games of ping-pong, and my athletic abilities showing out in tennis where I didn't return a single ball, I wished for the day to end. But a spark of our special friendship ignited with a furious card game we had played more than a thousand times—*Speed*.

However, my victory doused the flame.

Shuffleboard disks and sticks in hand, we tromped over the pine needles to the chipped blue concrete, the numbers faded to ailing lines.

I'd had it—tired, hungry, and sick of knowing he'd rather hang out with someone else. No bridge could be built over the gorge formed between us.

We heartlessly shoved the disks back and forth. Of course, Tim took the lead by double digits. My game was its usual mess. For every ten points I scored, twenty got deducted. With his score rising and mine plummeting from sight, I tried to salvage my attitude and prevent an explosion.

"Grrr, Tiggers don't like shuffleboard."

I had no idea why that particular statement bubbled out, and personally, I didn't think it was very funny. From the look my brother gave me, I figured my nutty sayings would always keep us apart.

Then he bent over double in laughter.

Tim spent the rest of the game pointing out my mistakes and showing me how to hold my shuffleboard stick properly. My score rose with my spirits.

Things changed after my impersonation of our childhood favorite Winnie-the-Pooh character. And with my talent in sports, I had plenty of opportunities to use it again. This time, I tried to choose the perfect moment.

When the ball bounced off my head, "Grrr, Tiggers don't like volleyball."

When the cue stick slipped from my fingers, "Grrr, Tiggers don't like shooting pool."

When my last arrow skittered through the dirt, "Grrr, Tiggers don't like archery."

Tim cracked up every time I used the silly phrase. I still

didn't get it, but I loved the warm fuzzies it produced when my brother repeated the story to others. The simple phrase created a connection between us, lost for so long.

And that's what Tiggers do the best.

Retiring Sam

Dawn came earlier than ever before. Or so it seemed to me.

Curled by the fireplace, I wanted more rest but the master was already stirring. I knew what I must face today. The air had a warm feeling—the time had come for cattle roundup.

"Come on, my good ole' Sam. The birds are chirping and the sun will be a' shinin'. Let's go boy, it's spring!"

The master's whistle had once sent a thrill of excitement through my body. Bounding past him, I would flash through the door before he could put on his worn cowboy hat.

Oh, how I loved running through the fresh sprigs of grass during roundup! One look at the master's face and I knew what to do. From nipping the heels of cattle to chasing strangers back to their cars, I took every part of my work serious.

I lived to please my master, and was often rewarded with a

scratch behind my ear as he spoke in the sweetest pitch, "That's my good ole' Sam. Don't know what I would do on this ranch without ya."

But this warm day was different. I whined softly as I struggled to stand. Each step to the master's side was more difficult than tackling an angry bull.

I studied my master's face, his sadness soaking through me. He squatted down, cupping my head in his well-calloused hands. His voice was soft. "Well, ole' Sam, I know this was a long winter for ya. I've seen ya struggling just following me to the barn. Thought the feeling of spring might perk you up."

He sighed. "I wanted to believe our bodies would give out at the same time. But you always did work twice as hard as me."

I sniffed at his hands, the familiar scent of bacon on them. He pulled a piece from the pocket of his denim shirt, and I lapped it off his fingers. "You did your job well, and now I reckon it's time for your retirement. There's no shame in it. Actually, life'll be easier for you, lying around the porch, chasing squirrels whenever you want. I'll sure miss having you by my side though. My good ole' Sam."

Though I could not understand all the master's words, I understood the pitch he used; so sad it made me whimper deep in my throat. I licked his hand and laid my head on his knee with my own sigh.

~~~

Stay was the only command the master gave me during the warm days when I tried following him to the truck every morning. Watching him drive away, I whined in confusion. Each day became more difficult for me to get on my feet.

Then a familiar green car rumbled up the dirt driveway to a stop in front of the house.

"Grandpa, Grandma!" the little carrot-topped miss called as she climbed out of the car. My tail wagging, I slowly followed the master and mistress to greet her.

"Good o' Sam!" Carrot Top squealed, grabbing my ears in a way that had once been so annoying. But for that moment, I acted like a young pup again.

~~~

Later that day as I lay resting on the porch, my ears pricked to catch the slight noise. The screen door swung out slowly. Carrot Top tiptoed over to me, and patted my head while my throat vibrated.

"Shhh, Sam, Grandma thinks I'm nappin'. I'm gonna pick her some flo'ers."

I cocked my head when Carrot Top disappeared around the barn. Instinct told me something was wrong. Carrot Top never went anywhere alone.

Tired as I was, I scrambled to my feet and limped to a trot, sensing danger.

Behind the barn I spotted Carrot Top picking the sweet smelling flowers. Another step, and the hair on my body tensed. When Carrot Top reached for a bright yellow flower her hand nearly brushed a copperhead snake.

Barking, I leaped between Carrot Top and the copperhead. She screamed and toppled backward. Teeth bared, I attacked the snake and moments later, it was dead.

"Melissa!" The mistress called out, and she scooped the weeping child into her arms. Seeing the dead snake under my front paws, the mistress began crying. I cocked my head.

Shouting, the master appeared and rushed over, wrapping his arms around them. Then the master looked at me. My tail wagged when I saw his pleased face.

"That's my good ole' Sam!"

His caressing hand rubbed behind my ears, and I leaned into it. "Here I thought it was time to put you out to pasture. But I see your most valuable work is only beginning."

Through the loving pitch of his voice, I knew exactly what my master said.

A merry heart does good, like medicine…

Proverbs 17:22

It Could Be Worse

The Orange Brigade

I kicked out my right foot, sending a spray of snow through the air. My left foot glided loose until the ski tips drew parallel to the mountainside, bringing my downhill flight to a halt.

Lifting my goggles, I gazed at the beauty of the Colorado Rockies stretching out of sight. The snow-capped mountains on the chiseled ranges mesmerized me. I leaned forward and relaxed on my ski poles. So breathtaking and serene…

Frantic shouts jolted me. "Brittney Ann, slow down!"

"Daddy, I can't stop!"

"Look at Brittney, Daddy, she's gonna fall!"

"Both of you just *stop*!"

I looked uphill at the chaos flying toward me. I didn't know whether to panic or laugh.

Two little girls struggled to stay upright while their dad tried to cut them off. Their unifying color of orange splotched my vision. Orange ski bibs, orange toboggans, orange gloves, orange goggles…this dad wasn't going to lose track of his kids.

"Watch out, Daddy! Move!"

The littlest one tumbled head over heels, her sister following suit. Dad went down last. The orange-ness disappeared in clouds of white.

A giggle suppressed, I called, "Everyone all right?"

An orange hand waved through the settling snow. "We're fine—it's all powder!"

~~~

Over the next few days, the "Orange Brigade" gained a reputation on the slopes. The mountainside café buzzed with the latest stories as I settled with my friends at a large round table. Hot soup warmed me, though I almost choked while eavesdropping on the anecdotes from a nearby table.

"Not a one of them have ever been on skis before," a robust man in a full black and red ski suit said. "They plowed all over the mountain this morning, and near took out a ski school when they accidently went down a Blue. You shoulda heard them little girls screaming! They were having a blast."

"Wait 'til you hear this," a young woman at the same table chimed in. "I was in the mountainside store getting new goggles when they tromped in. One of the little girls was crying. He bought her a new pair of pants, and I could tell from the conversation she didn't quite make it to the restroom in time."

"Maybe that's why I heard him walking down the trail to the parking lot, howling, 'Little girls for sale, little girls for sale!'"

Finishing off the soup, my friends and I prepared to hit the slopes again. We had to straighten our faces as we passed the Orange Brigade dragging into the café for a late lunch. The only thing not orange about them were their faces. They didn't know that you do indeed need sunscreen, even in 20-degree temperatures.

~ ~ ~

Both poles in one hand, I glided down the slope ahead of my friends on our last run of the day. Camera in my other hand, I spun a one-eighty to face uphill. "Smile!"

I snapped the picture, and then my friends continued past me while I struggled with my backpack zipper.

"Excuse me!"

Uphill, the Orange Brigade skied toward me. Somehow, they all managed to stop in unison.

"Could you take our picture and email it to me?"

"Sure, no problem." *Perfect for our trip album too.* "Got it."

I gulped when they started downhill again, three sets of ski tips pointed straight at me. I breathed a prayer of thanks when they skittered to stop just inches away.

"Sorry," the dad said as he awkwardly balanced himself. "Do you have something to write down my email address?"

"Uh, I don't…wait, I can use my cell." Extracting it from around old tissues and Slim Jim wrappers in my zippered coat pocket, I quickly added the info.

The dad puffed a sigh of relief. "Thanks. We dropped our camera from the lift the first day, and my cell, uh…well it's gone too."

"No problem. Glad you guys enjoyed skiing, and no injuries, huh?"

"A miracle," he muttered before giving his troops their marching orders. "Okay girls, this is our last run. Let's make that goal of getting all the way down with nobody falling."

"Daddy, I gotta go to the bathroom!"

I snapped one last picture of the Orange Brigade careening topsy-turvy down the Colorado Rocky mountainside.

Too Clever

I drew the short straw.

After the blow up seven years ago about moving great-aunt Edna to an assisted living facility, a family vote was taken last week to move her—this time, without asking. All the arrangements had been made, but no one wanted to be the one to scheme the actual transportation, and since I'd dropped out of college last semester, the family dumped it on me.

Auntie didn't say much at my phone call that her not-so-favorite great-niece wanted to stay with her a few days. I could only hope that at ninety-six, she didn't still remember the broken china doll incident when I was twelve.

I arrived, and we ate a light supper. She went to bed before dark. I could scarcely hold my pulsating heart at how easy my plan was falling into place. I'd have her packed and moved to

Shady Willows Assisted Living before she knew what happened.

Sitting with legs crossed on the musty shag carpet, about a thousand steps overdue for a cleaning, I doubled over and pulled VHS tapes from the low shelf of the living room bookcase. John Wayne's *The Searchers* stacked next to a dubbed copy of *Gone With the Wind*. *Abbott and Costello* and *The Three Stooges* would keep her grinning as she adjusted to her new home. Just two more tapes near the back…

Steel fingers gripped my shoulder. I squealed before flushing the guilt from my face. I looked up to meet Aunt Edna's eyes. From this angle, the half-bent woman seemed disproportionate in every way. I stuttered.

"I—I thought you were asleep."

Auntie didn't focus on the box filled with her possessions. "I was, darling, but those cats are fighting outside under my window again, making such a racket."

Her voice cracked, but I had my doubts as to Auntie's frailty as the blood vessels in my shoulder flattened in the car-crusher grip.

"There's a spray bottle full of water on the counter by the back door. A few squirts will send them critters running. Would you be a darling and go take care of it? I need my rest so bad."

I grabbed for the arm of the recliner, scrambling to my feet. My fingers clutched the afghan draped across it. A flip of the wrist sent it over the box. Perfect. "Sure, Auntie. You go on back to bed now; I'll lock up." I patted the elderly woman's arm.

Aunt Edna nodded and, still bent, used the recliner and coffee table to propel herself before disappearing down the hall.

Heavy cloud cover in the night sky made me glad for the soft beam of the old flashlight I had grabbed with the spray bottle. I bounced down the porch steps and flashed the beam under one of Auntie's bedroom windows. Nothing. I rounded the corner to the other window. The quiet of the country neighborhood wrapped around me.

"Well, that was fun."

I skipped the back porch steps and landed in front of its door, hand extended. I hadn't planned on stopping. I was forced to.

Locked. Now how did that happen? Another jiggle on the knob confirmed.

Not one to waste time on a lost cause, I jogged around to the front. Same result.

"You gotta be kidding."

I leaned on the doorbell, the ancient chimes sounding through the house, and remembered how long it'd taken Auntie to make it to the front door earlier that day. I pictured her shuffling through the house, balancing herself with a touch to everything, turning on lights as she came. All this after she put on her robe and slippers.

Minutes ticked by.

Back around the side of the house, I rapped on Aunt Edna's window. No lights flickered, and it occurred to me the house held a strange darkness. Hadn't I left the kitchen and living room lights on?

Surely at least one window was open. I started with the back of the house and made my way around the side opposite Aunt Edna's room, keeping a constant watch for signs of intelligent life.

Stretched over the bushes, I rattled the front window, wincing. Rose thorns scratched my bare stomach as my sweat-shirt lifted. It was this graceful position the spotlight caught me in.

"Freeze, police!"

Oh, did I freeze. It couldn't get any better than this. Especially since I looked the part of an escaped convict in my old gray sweat suit no one but Auntie was supposed see me in. I hadn't even bothered with makeup that morning.

An embarrassing eternity later, I stood on the front porch, flanked by two policemen. One of them, Officer Rogers, rang the doorbell.

"It may take her a minute," I said, trembling. "She's really hard of hearing…"

I left off my sentence as the light progression flashed from the back area of the house all the way to the front porch. Amazing. Why hadn't she answered ten minutes ago?

The door cracked open. Officer Rogers spoke. "Ma'am, we received a call about a prowler and found this young lady trying to get in one of your windows. Do you know her?"

I rolled my eyes and waited. Nothing.

"Auntie?"

Aunt Edna straightened to her full height of five-foot six and adjusted the rim of her ancients, studying me.

"No, Officer, I don't believe I do."

~~~

The next morning, after Mom bailed me out of jail and we were safely in her car, I had recovered from shock sufficiently enough to explode.

"I can't believe it. I just can't believe it!"

"Now, love, we'll get it all straight when we talk to Aunt Edna. I'm sure she was just confused last night."

"Confused? Mom, she had me arrested!"

"It is kinda funny…" I caught my mom's eye. She abandoned that sentence and started a new one. "We'll get all the charges dropped, and there won't even be a spot on your record."

My stomach lurched and I paled. Criminal record? I flopped my head back against the seat.

Half the neighbors peaked through their blinds at me. I wondered which rat had called the police.

Auntie had a tea tray, complete with homemade cookies, set on her coffee table when we entered the unlocked front door at her bidding. "Come on in here, darlings."

My voice tipped on screeching.

"Okay, Aunt Edna, why did you tell the police I wasn't your niece?"

"I never said that."

Her calm demeanor unnerved me. Where was the senile old lady I'd come to haul away?

"But you…I, uh, they—"

"It felt terrible, didn't it?" Auntie settled in her brown recliner, draping the afghan over her legs. The box I had filled with the VHS tapes was gone. "Being locked out, no one hearing your cries for help, or acknowledging you for who you are?"

I blinked and dropped on the blue sofa next to Mom. "You locked the back door and called the police, didn't you?"

In spite of the avalanche of wrinkles, Aunt Edna's smile was unmistakably catty. "I'm sorry, darling, but I had to. I knew the truth the minute you called. Y'all had a big family meeting about me, didn't you?" The gentle accusation was directed toward Mom, who developed a sudden interest in thumb twiddling.

"Now, Auntie—"

"The only thing wrong with having a meeting about me is having one without me."

Aunt Edna tilted her head back to me. "You came to move my life right out from under me without a word. Well, God put it on my heart that you had some lessons to learn, young lady. I think we all did. I know I haven't been the most sociable in the family but—but there are reasons for that." Auntie stared into the fireplace where a basket of fake floral took residence in the summer.

What secret pains and heartaches did that old heart hold? I didn't know my great aunt at all. Perhaps no one in the family did. Perhaps I was the one who should dig deeper.

"I'm sorry, Auntie. Believe me, I've learned my lesson."

Aunt Edna came back to the present. "All this fuss and for nothing. It's about time I moved out of this place. Too much upkeep anymore. Think your Uncle Herman could find a nice little retirement home for me?"

The catty smile was back and I actually enjoyed eye contact with my aunt as she said, "I just seemed like a little old lady to you, but after last night, how do you see me?"

A mix between a chuckle and a snort deflated the last of the irritation bundled in my stomach. I shook a finger at Aunt Edna. "A clever young lady."

Auntie snuggled the afghan around her knees and leaned back in her recliner.

"We're not so different, are we?"

A Different Breed

The rutty dirt drive meandered through the cowboy church's parking lot. That was Nicole's first hint she was in for a whole new experience, and the next two hints came right after—a metal building with its wide wrap around concrete porch and an abundance of pickup trucks with trailer hitches.

Stephen parked right in front, ramping up Nicole's apprehension. She stayed motionless, watching the regulars file by and enter through the double glass doors. Most wore jeans and western shirts, including the ladies. Only one woman in a skirt, though it was offset by the straw hat planted on her black curls. Nicole smoothed the floral print of her new Easter dress and realized she was tapping the toe of her black high-heel on the floorboard.

"Ready, girls?" Stephen was oblivious to her discomfort with the cultural differences as he opened his door. Nicole sighed and rolled her eyes, keeping her head tilted so her daughters in the backseat wouldn't see.

Moments later, Nicole scrunched up her nose when it was assaulted by the smell of manure as they passed a circle of cowboys on the porch. It was impossible to sidestep the manure-booted man without coming face-to-face with him as he turned from his conversation. He tipped up the brim of his weather-beaten cowboy hat and spit in the Styrofoam cup he gripped in a gnarled hand. Nicole wished she hadn't seen the drippings he swiped clean with the back of his sleeve as he continued the conversation. "'Fore she died, Mama made me promise to always be in church on Easter Sunday. Never liked them suit-and-tie churches. I'm glad ol' Rex here invited me out this mornin'. Why the—"

"Watch your step, girls." Nicole hoped her loud tone would drown out the man's swearing. Her ears burned. She guided her daughters around the entrance congestion.

They entered the sanctuary, if she could call it one. Rows of cushioned metal chairs lined the center of the open room, while long white folding tables occupied the side walls where one could sit with a nice view of the pasture land parking lot. Exposed iron beams contrasted the white insulation of the ceiling and interior walls. Unpainted wood walls sectioned off two restrooms and a kitchen area.

Stephen made a clear path to a vacant back row. Hands on her two daughters' shoulders, Nicole navigated them to the seats. She guided the girls to sit between her and Stephen as she eyed the people.

"Mom," Alexis whispered as the first tingle of guitar music drifted through the speakers, "I thought you weren't supposed to wear hats in church?"

Oh, why couldn't there be a nice *regular* church in this hick town? Why had moving to the quiet country seemed such a romantic idea a year ago?

Nicole shook her head in response to Alexis, and then angled it sideways to eye her husband. He wasn't bothered in the least. In fact, a content smile played on his lips as he watched the settling congregation. It confirmed her suspicion—he'd spent too much time hanging out in that feed store, dreaming of becoming a farmer. Rancher. Cowboy. Whatever.

Spurs jingled louder than the opening song, and the smell of manure captured Nicole's breath as she watched the tobacco chewing cowboy park himself two seats upwind of her.

Too late for musical chairs, Nicole resorted to praying. *Lord, You know I would do anything You ask. Really. Be a missionary in China. Put up with an atheist neighbor. Walk barefoot across the desert to give a cup of water to the weary. But God, please don't have me sit next to this vile smelling…I mean, um, this, uh, cowboy. I'm not being judgmental, but it's just—it's the smell, Lord. Terrible for my respiratory system, I'm sure. And it is Easter Sunday. Please do something. Now.*

The sermon began. Nicole mechanically opened her Bible and searched for the passages the pastor referred to, but it was impossible to concentrate on his message. Not that it could be much different from the dozens of Easter sermons she'd heard since childhood.

The noxious fumes continued and Nicole's breathing plummeted as she swayed. She'd never fainted but this experience would make a memorable first. The pastor wrapping up his sermon strengthened her.

"It's really that simple, folks," he said. "Jesus died on the cross for your sins and was raised again on the third day. If you were the only person on this earth, He'd have done it for you. You can pray this simple prayer right here and get saved. Ask Jesus into your heart today…"

Nicole knew she'd never survive the closing prayer, head bowed and nothing to do but sniff manure. It filtered through her lips, the taste gagging her.

The girls' stretched-out legs with crossed ankles blocked a gracious escape to the right, leaving an undesirable alternative. Nicole eased herself around and closed her Bible, a polite "excuse me" ready on her lips.

Her eyes traveling up from the mud splattered boots, Nicole realized the genuine cowboy's head was bowed. The pastor began the salvation prayer. The man's face drew up earnestly as his lips moved, repeating it word for word.

Nicole leaned back and dipped her head with closed eyes. Maybe the smell wasn't so bad.

I'm Just Sayin'

I watch the corners of her mouth. That's where the first signs always appear. A slight twitch, lips tighten, corners bend down just a touch.

After I read all I can from her lips, my eyes move up to hers. Focused, unblinking, scanning a single sentence a dozen and one times. When her brows knit together, I know something major is coming. I pretend to busy myself reading another copy while I search her face for further signs. I finally speak.

"Well?" I count the seconds. The longer her reply takes, the worse the answer.

"Hmmm." My editor never says much at first. I try to swallow my impatience.

"What do you think? Any good, or should I just throw it out and start over?" I'm careful not to say too much. My editor can lose her train of thought rather easily sometimes.

"Well, let's see." Another long pause. Her slow response is brutal. I suppress a sigh as I wiggle slightly in my chair.

"So you don't like it?"

"I didn't say that."

"But it's what you want to say."

"It's not that I don't like it. It's just this one part that's bugging me."

"What's that?"

"Well…"

I resist putting a hand on top of my head to keep it from exploding.

"It's just this part about the brother coming home. I mean, he gets on a bus and his sister just happens to be at the bus stop when he gets there? It doesn't seem realistic."

I squirm. "But that's the whole gist of it. She goes to the station every day, hoping he'll come. She almost doesn't go that day, but something prompts her to. That's why I had that phone call in there, to show what was going on instead of telling it."

"Well, I'm just saying, it doesn't quite work. Something isn't flowing right. Maybe you could have it where she runs into him at the hospital where he finally arrives to see their dying father. I mean, that *is* why she's hoping he'll come. Then you can tie that whole scene together and save word count. You have to keep it under three thousand and you're at three thousand eighty-six."

I avoid my editor's eyes. *But I want them to meet at the bus station. Otherwise, I have to figure out how to squeeze that wise bystander into the hospital scene and that won't work. Or will it?*

"So," I say, "you think the woman who talks to them about God could be at the hospital instead of catching a bus to reunite with her husband? Why would she be at the hospital?"

"Hmmm."

I continue, "Okay, how about this: the sister is about to leave the hospital for the day and runs into her brother in the parking lot. The woman could be a nurse at the hospital and that's where she meets them on her way to leave for the bus station."

My editor's mouth twists to one side. After working with her for nearly twenty years, I know it's a definite sign she isn't getting the picture—or doesn't like what she sees. I must wait for her feedback without speaking.

"That might work. What about the phone call and all of that?"

"It can still be a part of it. I'll just add another twist." My words are more confident than my feelings.

After an hour of re-work, I once again study my editor's face for honest reaction. I see her focus on one line. I know the problem.

"You don't like the word I used there, do you? 'Reserved' for the sister's reaction?"

"Well, I think we could find a better one." And we do. Half an hour later.

Suffering from emotional exhaustion following the roller coaster story I've produced, I prop my head up with one hand before asking, "What do you think? Is it getting close?"

"Well, what about…"

Two more hours pass. My editor's stamina and patience never cease to amaze me.

"This is looking really good." I sit up straighter at the first praise of my piece. My editor's words carry me through the next hour of tweaking and proofreading.

"I think it's ready. You've written a great story, Lu."

Beaming, I wrap my arms around my editor's neck and kiss her cheek.

"Thank you, Mama. I couldn't do it without you."

Of Pies & Pastors

Six months after the wedding vows, I wondered if our marriage could handle one more *oops*.

I flooded the basement of our new house. Cynthia broke the zipper on her formal dress five minutes *after* we were supposed to be at a banquet. Backing my truck over her cat didn't help the building tension. Then there was the case of salt-instead-of-sugar in her brownies. I gagged. Cynthia sobbed the whole night.

Things brightened the day my little wife's apple pie came out tasting like my mama's. I heaped compliments on Cynthia as we polished off all but one piece.

With the apple pie success, confidence built—until our pastor dropped by right at suppertime.

Cynthia called me into the kitchen during dinner. Her face was ghost white as she snagged my arm, her fingernails digging in like a five pronged fish hook. "I only have one piece of apple pie left to serve for dessert. What am I going to do? This is so embarrassing."

"Hey, honey, it's not so bad. There's some ice cream in the freezer. We'll just have it with chocolate syrup…" The look in Cynthia's eyes left my sentence hanging.

An idea illuminated her face. "Here's what we'll do. When I offer dessert, you say you don't want any, I won't have any, and we'll give the last piece to the pastor."

Thankfully, she didn't hear my half-hearted approval as she spun back through the swinging kitchen door.

"My, my, Cynthia, that was a wonderful meal." Pastor turned to me. "Carl, how did you end up with such a beautiful wife plus a marvelous cook?"

I opened my mouth, but it filled with Cynthia's words. "Would you care for a slice of apple pie, Pastor?" She rose like a princess and removed his dinner plate.

"Thank you, but no. One more bite and I wouldn't be able to preach for a month of Sundays!"

If I hadn't let loose a polite chuckle, I might have realized in time I needed to keep my mouth shut. But that apple pie called my name.

"Honey, I believe I'll have a piece."

I almost missed her look when she set the dessert plate in front of me. I shoved the second bite in my watering mouth when the pastor dropped the bomb with my death sentence.

"You know, Cynthia, that pie looks so good, I believe I will have a piece."

My wife's glare singed my eyebrows. I listened for her to breathe. She didn't.

Rescuing my wife at that moment should have scored as downright chivalrous, but seeing my part in the sticky mess, I knew my motives were purely of self-preservation.

I gulped and met the pastor's eyes. "Well sir, uh, Pastor, to be honest, this was the last piece. I thought since you didn't care for any—uh, well, I just didn't want it go to waste."

A smile spread across our guest's face as he took in the situation. The smile turned to a chuckle then a booming laugh. I knew right then we were sermon material.

I chatted with the pastor awhile before seeing him out.

On tiptoe, I peeked through the kitchen door. Cynthia stood at the sink, sliding dishes in with a clang. Her shoulders shook.

I didn't feel I could handle her tears at one more *oops*. But what choice did I have?

I put my hands on her arms and turned her around, letting the sudsy water drip from her hands onto my ostrich boots. I opened my mouth to speak, but she cut me off with a burst of hysterical laughter. That's when I knew I had driven her over the edge.

"Sweetheart, it's okay." I squeezed her arms and bent my knees to get eye level. "It was my fault. If I hadn't asked for that last piece–"

"Then we wouldn't be laughing at ourselves!"

Sucking air with a hiccup, Cynthia dabbed the corners of her eyes with my shirt. "Aren't we silly? We've been pretending to know what marriage is all about. We just need to be patient and grow together, and stop getting worked up over the little things."

Relieved, I leaned forward and touched my nose to hers. "I agree with you whole heartedly, Mrs. Nelson." I would have given my wife a little kiss if I hadn't looked over her shoulder at the overflowing sink.

Oops.

Sermon Material

"While they went to buy, the bridegroom came, and those who were ready went in with him to the wedding; and the door was shut. Afterward the other virgins came also, saying, 'Lord, Lord, open up to us!' But he answered and said, 'Assuredly, I say to you, I do not know you.'"

Our pastor looked up from his Bible and swept the congregation with his eyes. He leaned forward with both hands on the pulpit. His smile was teasing. "I recently witnessed a prime example of someone getting caught unprepared. It was on the day I visited the home of a couple from our church."

My stomach flipped and Cynthia slid a little lower in the pew. She caught on to the coming message as fast as I did.

Pastor Greg continued. "I won't name names, but let's just say they haven't been married for long." A chuckle rippled through the congregation of less than two hundred. Cynthia's head dipped below my shoulder.

"I dropped by one evening, and they invited me to stay for dinner. After the meal, the missus offered me dessert. Well, you all know how I watch my pie intake." Pastor Greg patted his ample waist, triggering more laughter. "I politely refused. But when her husband decided to have a piece of that sweet smelling homemade apple pie—well, I'm only made of flesh. So I asked for a piece."

Struggling to keep a straight face, Pastor Greg rested his elbows on the pulpit. I wondered if Cynthia would slide herself all the way to the floor.

"You would've thought I'd rolled a bowling ball down the middle of the table," Pastor Greg said. "That sweet couple looked at each other and the mister finally 'fessed up that there had only been one piece of pie left."

Pastor Greg waited for the laughter to settle. "I believe I know of two people who will always be prepared for the coming of the Lord—and their pastor."

After the service, I waited until we were in the parking lot before I said anything.

"Well, at least he didn't use our names."

"Humph! Did he have to?"

"Hey, Cynthia, it wasn't so bad. Look on the bright side—we can stop worrying about him actually using our little mishap for a sermon."

Cynthia stopped and twisted her mouth to the side as she glared at me. I reached out and pushed her nose with the tip of my finger. She fought it hard, but a smile tickled her lips and she giggled. I draped an arm around her and reached with the other hand to open the passenger door of our truck. The handle popped.

"Oops, guess I need the keys, huh?" I slid my free hand in my pocket. It met emptiness. I smiled at Cynthia and reached in my other pocket. Same result.

Her polished fingernail tapping glass froze me. "That what you're looking for?"

I didn't need to follow her finger to know where my truck keys were. I chuckled nervously. "Now, honey, everyone makes mistakes…"

"Humph!"

I knew the smile button trick wouldn't work a second time.

A familiar voice saved me—sort of. "Cynthia, Carl!"

We turned to see our pastor trotting toward us, holding out Cynthia's Bible.

"Oh, uh, thank you, Pastor Greg." The look on Cynthia's face was priceless, but I knew it would cost my life to say so.

Pastor Greg looked from my sheepish smile to Cynthia's scarlet face. "Everything all right?" He gazed past us to the truck. A knowing grin crinkled the corners of his eyes.

"Keys locked inside?"

Neither of us needed to answer. Pastor Greg cleared his throat. "I'll call a locksmith."

As our pastor walked away, the shaking of his shoulders confirmed we had again provided sermon material.

I tapped a finger on the leather cover of Cynthia's Bible. "If you hadn't left this…"

Cynthia cocked her head and batted her eyelashes. "We all make mistakes."

"Humph!"

Cynthia reached up and pushed my nose. My grin preceded hers as I bent to smack her lips.

Let Pastor Greg turn *that* into a sermon.

Can You
Hear Me Now?

"Does this dress look good on me?" Cynthia asked.

"Hmm," I murmured.

Her growl brought my eyes up from my notes and straightened me off the bedroom doorjamb. "What?"

"'Hmm' is not an answer. Did you even hear what I said?"

"Of course."

"Well?"

"I didn't say it don't look good."

"You didn't say it does either."

Before I could protest, Cynthia had tossed the garment on the massive pile covering our queen sized bed. She disappeared into the closet.

"Sweetie, I need to be at the men's Bible study early this morning or at least on time. Otherwise Pastor Greg will never ask me to lead it again."

No response. I dodged behind my shaking notes.

"Carl? Are you going to answer me?"

A quick look at my watch told me I needed to play the enthusiasm card. "Yeah, Baby, it does."

Her eyebrows bushed together. I gulped and asked, "What?"

"I just asked if this dress made me look fat."

A tornado roaring through the house would help, but a car horn saved me instead.

"Who could that be?" Cynthia stretched over the window seat to peer out, one bare foot stuck out behind her.

"Honey, I gotta go. I asked your mom to swing by and pick you up if we hadn't left yet…"

Cynthia swung around and a look I couldn't quite place filled her blueberry eyes. "But—"

A knock at the door interrupted her. I smacked a kiss on my little wife's forehead, scooting away before she could fuss about how I smeared her make-up.

"I'll see you at church." The edge of the door frame met my face. I bounced off it and ran through the living room to let my rescuer in.

My mother-in-law. My hero.

~~~

"Glad you made it, Carl." A grin split Pastor Greg's face as he glanced at the wall clock of the small room reserved for the men's Sunday morning Bible study.

I shook the pastor's hand with a stiff smile, grateful my neck was already beet red from haying all the day before. Somehow, I was able to hold my notes and Bible steady enough to present the devotion.

~~~

"How do I look?" Cynthia whispered as we bumped through the crowded aisle to our usual middle row in the sanctuary.

"Baby, I told you at the house, that dress is great on you."

She pinned her lips.

"This isn't the same dress."

Our fathers were near tears as they suppressed their laughter during the opening worship service.

When everyone stood after the final amen, Cynthia reached over and grabbed my hand. "Carl—"

"Great job this morning, Carl." Sims, a neighbor, pumped my hand.

When I pried away, I absently turned to Cynthia. "What is it, honey?"

"I—" She looked past me at the men waiting to talk. She sighed and shook her head. "I'm riding home with Mom."

After the handshakes and chit-chat, I caught up with my dad and learned Cynthia had already left.

"Guess I'd better get on home."

"I would." The twinkle in my dad's eye made me smile.

"You and Mama went through the same stuff, didn't you?"

"Yep."

"Does it get any easier?"

"Your guesswork improves."

Opening my truck door I grimaced at the objects lying in the seat. Grandpa's expired hearing aid and Granny's tiny spectacles.

"Okay, I get the message." I gingerly moved the antiques

to the passenger side, and hoisted myself into the crew cab. My eyes riveted to the rearview mirror. Or rather the object taped to it, dangling down as big as life. Literally.

An infant sized diaper smiled at me, a note protruding from one of its tiny leg openings. Scrawled in Cynthia's bold style were the words:

Can You Hear Me Now?

I got a speeding ticket on the way home. I just wished I'd remembered to take the diaper down.

Reaction

Four o'clock came too soon. Janis puffed her bangs skyward with a sigh. A new riding student started today, and her regular volunteer had cancelled at the last minute. It was up to her and the new girl, a wannabe junior dressage champ, to handle the class. Two volunteers had to quit for various reasons in the last month.

Janis speared her pencil into the *Horse Lover* coffee mug on her desk and reached for the scrapbook her students and parents had made her. This was her habit when she wondered why she continued living her dream of operating a therapeutic riding center. The scrapbook highlighted the multiple achievements of the Center and never failed to put a smile on Janis' face—but not today.

The office door opened, and Karlene appeared. Her ears were stopped with music so loud Janis understood the words. She closed the scrapbook with a thud and opened her mouth wide. "You'll need to leave your iPod here."

Karlene yanked one earphone out. "Why?"

"In class we need to focus on the student."

The other earphone came out and Karlene looked surprised. "Whoa, wait a second. You mean, like, I have to actually help with a class?"

Janis sighed. *God, please help me.* "Come out to the arena. We have things to do before the student arrives."

She led the way through the back door to the large indoor arena and stalls. The smell of freshly turned dirt didn't revive her spirit nor did she listen to the peaceful snort of horses as they greeted her from their stalls. She turned right and lengthened her stride. Karlene's shuffle sounded loud on the concrete aisle. They entered the tack room.

"Here's everything we need for classes. Not just tack, but game supplies used in aiding the physical therapy. Today we have a new student, James, who has Down syndrome. He's three years old."

Karlene sputtered. "I thought I was just helping with the horses—you know, like, grooming, feeding, riding. I didn't know I would have to, like, do anything with kids."

Janis lifted a tub of grooming supplies and placed it on her hip. "Don't worry—Dapples will teach all you need to know about working with kids." She nodded to a halter and lead rope hanging near the door. "Grab those and follow me." Karlene complied slowly.

She crossed her arms on the half door of the stall Janis had entered. "Who's Dapples?"

Janis set the box down and stroked the short neck of the dappled gray mare. "Meet Dapples. She's been with me four years and I couldn't ask for a better horse to start students—or volunteers—on."

"So…what do I do?"

"I'll go over the rules while we're tacking up. But there's something important I want you to watch for."

"What?"

Janis closed her eyes, thinking of her own volunteering years. How she wished for the passion she'd had then. Oh well. She'd have to get through another day without it. "Watch the first time James touches Dapples. Watch his reaction."

~~~

Prep work completed, Janis welcomed her new student and his mom into the arena. James seemed content in his mother's arms until his caught sight of Dapples. He drew back and cried out in fear.

His mom patted his back, concern on her face. Janis motioned Karlene to lead Dapples to them, and softened her voice. "James, this is Dapples. She's really sweet and wants to be your friend. Would you like to pet her?"

Janis gently took James' hand, moved it toward the large animal and helped his fingers touch the soft, well groomed hair. She guided until he stroked the stubby neck on his own. A giggle illuminated his face.

His mother transferred him to Janis' arms, and they stepped toward Dapples' nose. "See how big her eyes are, James? She's looking right at you!"

James' head rolled back, but Janis supported him as he found the balance to reach out and touch Dapples' nose.

Karlene stood in front of the horse, a hand on each side of the halter just as instructed, but Janis didn't like what she read on the teen's face. *She won't be here long.* Discouragement filled Janis.

Twisting, James reached out and touched Karlene's cheek as another giggle sounded. A half smile turned to a full one as Karlene's shoulders relaxed and she met Janis' eyes. "Cool," she mouthed.

Janis basked in the joy returning to her heart. The dream was still worth living.

A Coke, Dr Pepper &
Two Kids Later

Arthur rocked his foot again to keep the porch swing in a steady rhythm. One hand rested on his son Tommy's shoulder as the little boy lay across his lap, asleep. Arthur's other arm stretched behind Alma, lightly touching her shoulders. The blonde curls of little Mary's sleeping head tumbled over Alma's knees and swayed with the movement of the swing. Arthur sighed. Nothing could beat this cool spring evening.

Alma's weight shifted with her own sigh. "You know something, Arthur?"

"Hmmm?" he murmured, leaning his head back to watch the speckle of moonlight through the branches of the oak tree. He inhaled the crisp air saturated with honeysuckle.

"In the seven years we've been married, you ain't once said

you loved me."

Arthur lifted his head and stared at her. "I ain't?"

"Nope. Not once." Her dark chocolate eyes were melting.

Arthur let his gaze return to the oak tree moonlight. He tried to think back on the time he first saw Alma, but couldn't bring it to mind. He did recall the long weeks that passed where he sat in the corner booth of the town's only café and watched Alma come from her courthouse clerking job to eat lunch every day. He would hold the newspaper in front of his face until she left. There were times he just knew she glanced his way. But they never spoke until the day the waitress, whose smile was as slender as her frame, brought him a Dr Pepper with a wink.

"Young lady at the counter bought this for you." She stepped to the side and nodded at the wide open chocolate brown eyes. Arthur gulped. "She did?"

"Uh-huh." The waitress winked again before moving to the next table of the lunch hour rush.

Though his hand shook, Arthur picked up the hard plastic cup and walked the straightest line he could toward the chocolate brown eyes. "Uh, thanks for the Dr Pepper, but I, uh, really like Coke."

The eyes widened. "I didn't—" She cocked her head to look around him and he turned to see the slender smile radiating across the room. Arthur's cheeks flamed. "Uh…"

"Here." The chocolate eyed girl handed Arthur her drink. "This is the Coke you bought me—uh, I like Dr Pepper myself."

Wind jostled the oak tree branches, revealing the full moon. Arthur squeezed the warm flesh of his son's shoulder. A soft snore vibrated up to his ears.

Arthur gazed into his wife's chocolate eyes. "Sorry about

that, Alma. I guess it's because—well, I love you the way God loves."

"Huh?"

"You know. Like eternity. No real beginning." He nodded resolutely. "And it sure ain't ever gonna end."

Now her eyes did melt. "Guess that's as good as it gets."

When he leaned in to put some sugar on her cheek, Arthur swore he tasted the fizzy flavor of Coke.

Known to God from eternity are all His works.
Acts 15:18

Humanity's Path

Misconceptions

The black top hat and neatly trimmed mustache set the man apart from the native folk of the small town. Wide circles were made around him and whispers from the town gossips abounded.

"Who you suppose he is?"

"I heard he's one of them government men."

"Nah, he'd shoved papers in someone's face afore now."

"He's got plenty of paper, for sure."

"Martin at the hotel says his name is John Piton, and he's a writer for one of them big Boston newspapers. He's wanting to do a story about the growing West and—"

"You think you know everything, Thelma. So happens I talked to Burt at the general store and he says Mr. Piton is here to write about them—"

The writer stepped onto the porch of the hotel, silencing the gossips. A pad was tucked under his arm and a pencil twirled in his fingers.

A distant figure was running up the muddy road. A minute later, the young boy slid to a halt in the middle of Main Street, waving to the sheriff.

"They're coming," the boy gasped, pointing. "They're taking 'em this way after all. You gonna let 'em stop in town?"

Thumbs hooked in his vest, the sheriff leaned back on his boot heels and shook his head at the gathering crowd. "I don't reckon we have to worry about them stopping here. Too much daylight left."

The icy winter wind reflected the feelings of the towns-people as the gathering crowd moved to the mouth of their domain. The road forked at the edge of the last building and the human barricade left only one way.

Pad in hand, the writer left the hotel porch and walked to the point of the fork. He stood there alone, eyes on the road where the dark cluster grew. He was oblivious to the fingers pointing his way and the idle chatter of those in the crowd. In the moment, the only thing of interest to him was the long train of human beings in a slow march.

The first wagon rolled by. No sounds came from the townspeople. They seemed content in leaving the marchers alone provided they got the same.

The writer sketched the first reddish brown face. The man moved solemnly, a carved walking staff preceding his steps. When he reached the writer, the man turned to face his people as they moved past the town.

The writer opened his mouth, but paused. The man's face was withered with more than age. Though his head was held high, his shoulders sagged slightly in—what? Weariness? Defeat? Hopelessness?

A shout came from the crowd. "Hey, don't leave that one

behind!"

A small boy stood to the side of the line of marchers. Two fingers were in his mouth as he rubbed one bare foot on top of the other. Tears glistened on his cheeks before the freezing wind dried them.

Trotting past astride his horse, a uniform clad man shouted, "His folks drowned when we crossed the river. Don't worry; one of the squaws will pick him up."

However, it was not one from the line of marchers, but a townswoman who stepped forward and wrapped the child in her shawl. She held the boy close until a young woman from the march approached and took him in her arms. The townswoman secured the shawl around him with a loose knot.

As the young woman passed the writer, she murmured to the child in a sing-song voice. The writer's eyes focused on the blood caked to the bottom of the child's feet.

The writer continued sketching as his questions came. "Sir, how do you feel about the removal? Your people forced to leave their homes, their farms, all the bounty they knew in Mississippi?"

For a long moment, the elderly man did not speak. But when the last straggling members of the band passed, he said, "We must forgive."

A note scribbled. "How would you describe your journey?"

The silence stretched long between the two. An eagle feather wisped together with graying strands blown into the weather worn face.

"This has been a trail of tears and death."

The marchers faded in the distance and the townspeople dispersed in hushed conversations. The writer gazed at his scribbling and sketches.

That winter, in the year 1831, John Piton's story of the government's forced removal of the Choctaw people appeared in the Arkansas Gazette. Its title headlined the front page:

TRAIL OF TEARS

Author's note: For more history and stories about the Choctaw Trail of Tears, please see *TOUCH MY TEARS: Tales from the Trail of Tears*. Available on Amazon.

Lesson Learned

I clutched my full skirt in one hand as I pushed through the underbrush, relieved to finally catch sight of the blackberry bushes.

"Over here, child," a voice called. I lifted my skirts and sprinted to Aunt Ida's side.

"I'm sorry to be late, Aunt Ida," I said, catching her calloused hand in a squeeze. Her dark skinned face was shaded by a worn, hand woven straw hat that didn't hide her toothy smile. "That pesky Robert Trent held me up. He thinks he's old enough to come a courting me. I told him to wait 'til his britches grew as big as his head."

Aunt Ida gave my hand a loving squeeze and released it as she reached for a clump of blackberries at the end of a sagging vine. She clucked her tongue. "You says that now, Missy Samantha, but you just wait a couple of years. Massa Robert be a handsome young man by then."

I frowned. "Let's not talk about it. He made me late for our lesson and look, you have the basket half-full already. Let me take it."

Retrieving the McGuffey Reader from my apron pocket, I traded it for the straw basket. "We stopped on page thirty-two."

Aunt Ida opened the book and drew it close to her nose, then held it at arm's length. I giggled.

"Now, Aunt Ida, I know you have fine eyesight. Quit stalling and read the first word. Remember, sound it out, like mmm-mma—"

"Maybe." Aunt Ida plucked three blackberries from the bush with her free hand, dropping them in the basket.

I cast a sideways glance at her. "And the next word?"

"Mother."

Shaking my head, I pricked my finger as I reached for a berry. I popped the juicy morsel in my mouth. "You're smart, Aunt Ida. You're about the smartest person I know."

The older woman chuckled softly. "Oh child, I reckon there be a few folks you could put ahead o' me."

"Not many."

"You be pretty smart yourself."

My cheeks reddened. "No, I'm not. When I try to read music, the notes just dance all over the page…" I clamped my mouth shut.

Silence fell as we continued filling the basket. Aunt Ida broke it with her direct address.

"I know you hurting 'bout something. Last night, I leaves to get refreshments and when I come back, you done gone to your room. Why don't you tell ol' Ida about it?"

The basket weighed heavy on my trembling arm. "Papa wanted me to play the piano for the Thompsons, but it's hard when people expect so much. I sounded awful. Papa said I must not be feeling well and sent me to my room. I know I embarrassed him. He must hate me."

Aunt Ida's arms held me as the tears burst from my eyes.

"There, there, my child. You listen to Ida. Your papa don't hate you. He be mighty proud o' you, I know."

I pulled back, shaking my head, auburn curls slapping my face. "Ever since Mama died, Papa hasn't wanted me. I'll never be good enough. I don't know that I want to be." I twisted the ragged cloth Aunt Ida handed me, willing the tears to stop.

Aunt Ida's touch was gentle. "Listen here, Missy Samantha. Your papa be a hard man. But the good Lord says we is to love and respect our parents. 'Member reading me that from the good Book?"

I nodded. "But it isn't the same. God's strong. I'm weak. And I—I'm scared of Papa. He does bad things sometimes. Like the time Old Tinker forgot to latch the gate and Papa's stallion got out. Papa had him whipped, even though Tinker caught the horse. I can't be strong enough to always please him."

"You a strong girl, else you wouldn't be teaching me to read. Takes some bravery to do that. You could be in a heap o' trouble with the law for learning a slave woman her letters."

I frowned. "It doesn't take bravery, Aunt Ida. You're my friend. Besides, with you is the only time I'm not afraid."

Aunt Ida shook her head. "Child, when you have Jesus a living in you, you don't have to fear nothing. Why don't we pray and ask Him to he'p you?"

A lump rose in my throat. "It doesn't help. I pray, and go to church. I don't feel anything. I'm still afraid and hurting as much as ever."

"Going to church and praying ain't the same 'less you got Jesus in your heart." Aunt Ida's voice softened. "You know the difference, don't you, child?"

My gaze lingered on Aunt Ida. A glorious light illuminated her dark face, and pierced my soul. In an instant, I understood the true difference between me and the elder slave woman.

"I think I do."

My eyes went to the overflowing basket of blackberries. "Oh dear, the chore is done and we haven't finished the lesson!"

Aunt Ida slipped the worn McGuffey Reader into my apron pocket and lifted the basket. "Yeah, we have. We's all done with this lesson for now."

Be Proud

It rolled to a stop by the curb after school on a warm September day in 1963. Kids my age—some older, some younger—prowled around the odd-looking contraption. Oh, it had four wheels and a thunderous engine the same as any bus. But this one was different. White and blue, it didn't much resemble a school bus, especially with the large roll up door on its side and steps up to it.

I stood back, watching the other children giggle and poke one another until the side door of the peculiar bus rolled open.

The little group made a semi-circle. A funny yet wonderful smell drew me closer. The familiar face of my favorite teacher appeared.

"Which of you will dare enter the library bus first?" Ms. Perris asked, her eyes sparkling with mystery.

I found myself standing by the steps, ducking my head when I realized I was the only one. Snorts and chuckles burned the back of my neck.

Ms. Perris brushed away the sable brown strands escaping my ponytail. "Well, Mary Ann, looks like you get to be first. Hand your completed form to Mrs. Grimes and she'll give you a library card."

Schoolbooks snuggled close, I gladly slipped past Ms. Perris to the shelter of the smothering interior. I exchanged cards with Mrs. Grimes and she directed me.

The scent of hundreds of books made me shiver in pleasure as I raised my eyes to stare in wonder at the shelves and shelves of treasure. I had never known such a glorious world existed.

Hearing the pack of kids behind me, I hurried to the far corner and landed in the history section.

Absorbed among the giant shelves, I ran a finger along the titles, licking my lips in anticipation. Mrs. Grimes said we could choose up to five books each. Which would be mine?

No longer part of the present world, I thumbed the pages of illustrated history books. I stacked my favorites on the floor beside me: Daniel Boone, The Civil War, a collection of historical fiction, and tales of the Old West balanced together.

"Hola, como estas?"

I squirmed and met the eyes of the pretty Hispanic girl smiling at me. She was new at school, and probably looking to make friends. Swallowing, I spoke slowly, my Texas-Okie blended accent ringing true. "No speak Spanish."

The girl looked hard at me before scrunching her eyebrows and spinning away. I sniffed and coughed, convincing myself the dusty books had stirred up my allergies. There was no point in recalling how the Hispanic children thought I was one of them, only to be miffed when they heard my strange accent. They shunned me the same as the white kids did.

Focused on the shelf in front of me, I was determined to choose one more title. Surely I could find…

American Indians.

My fingers gripped the cover, but I hesitated. Memories of my fair-skinned classmates stared at me, and echoes of giggles and whispers rang in my car.

"Here comes Mary Ann, let's go."

"We don't want her to play with us."

"Pretend she isn't there."

Loosening my grip on the book, I turned to my stash. Four was enough.

"Be proud you're Indian."

My nose crinkled. Why did my daddy's words have to pop up right now? He didn't understand. He didn't know what it was like.

"Be proud."

The *American Indian* book tumbled off the shelf where I had pulled it half out, and it landed at my feet. Its front cover bounced open on impact and the pages split. I knelt and held it open with one finger.

A beautiful illustration filled my eyes. A young girl stood by the riverbank, her hand resting on a painted pony's neck.

"She looks like me," I whispered, turning the page. And another. And another. Buffalo, tepees, farms, rolling prairies, forests, children, fathers and mothers took me on a journey I wanted to remember.

God, this is how you created me.

I was the last to leave that heavenly library bus.

I will praise You, for I am fearfully and wonderfully made. Psalm 139:14 NKJV

Author's note: This fiction story is based on an accumulation of the author's mother's childhood experiences.

Names

Pavement flashed beneath the front bike tire. Faster, faster, faster I pumped. Slower, slower, slower I seemed to go. Sunbeams burned the back of my neck. I never was one to get out in the sun much, especially this summer. Who wanted the heat when you could sit in front of the TV all day eating ice cream and getting fat? At least that's what my one and only friend just told me. My ex-friend.

He used to be the only one who didn't make fun of me. Didn't call me a fatso and other stuff I stuff down and don't think about. The kids at school gave me nicknames that went with whatever I was eating.

"Hey fatty hamburger patty."

"Hey big belly jelly."

"Hey cream puff cheeks."

The next hill loomed and my calves burned. I couldn't make it, but I had to. Had to prove I could if I wanted.

Sweat ran into the corners of my mouth. The salty tang made me crave French fries. Or a bag of potato chips. Right now, though, a giant gulp of water would taste best. My tongue was swelling in proportion to the hill I was halfway up.

After I had stormed out in the middle of a movie at my ex-friend's house, I grabbed his bike, yelling at him that I could not eat for a week and lose all the weight I wanted to. Could ride the bike to the next state if I wanted.

I gasped for air, staring at the pavement of the neighborhood street I was pumping up. I'd never ridden a bike to or from my ex-friend's house before. The seven blocks seemed like miles. But I had to make it. Too late to turn back now.

Heat rushed through every pore on my face, the sides of my head pounded. I topped the hill but another one loomed. The bike quivered beneath me. My hands slipped from sweat and I gripped down on the handlebars. Spots danced on the pavement now, weird patterns of bright blues and reds on the dirty gray sidewalk.

An ocean of noise roared in my ears. The bike slowed. Cruel voices and names swirled around in my mind.

Then those noises faded and something else broke through.

"Andy!"

Someone called my name. My real name. I let the tips of my tennis shoes drag the pavement still dancing with blue and red dots.

"Andy? Are you okay?"

On the curb just ahead of me, a truck came to an abrupt halt and the driver hopped out. My ex-friend's dad, Mr. Adams. Tall, lean, built. The kind of dad who would take you to the gym and to church on Sundays. The kind I'd always wanted. If I had a dad. If mine hadn't died before I had a chance to remember him.

I hung my head rather than look at Mr. Adams as I muttered, "Sorry I took Payton's bike. I just wanted to go home."

"You look like you're about to pass out. Come on over to the truck."

I slowly dismounted the bike, and made my legs follow him, vaguely aware I'd let the bike fall to its side. I hoped it didn't get scratched up.

Mr. Adams held something in my still spotty vision. "Drink slow."

I took the mini Gatorade and sipped it like he said. I didn't want him to get mad at me. He didn't. "What's up, Andy?"

I shrugged. Suddenly, what Payton had said didn't seem cruel. He never meant to hurt me. He was my one and only friend.

"You want to come back to our house and finish the movie? Payton paused it."

All I could do was nod and drain the last of the Gatorade while he put Payton's bike in the bed of his truck.

On the short drive back, Mr. Adams said, "Before school starts up again, I promised Payton I'd take him to the gym and teach him safe ways to work out. You could come along, if it's okay with your mom. But we'll be going at 5:30 in the mornings. Think you can handle that?"

An air conditioned gym. I glanced out the window at the flying pavement and heat. "Yes, sir."

"I think you'll like the strawberry protein shakes I make." Mr. Adams winked at me. I grinned. Who knew but by the time school started I'd have a new tasty nickname, like Muscle Milkshake.

I could do it—with a little help.

I Didn't
Know You Were...

My fingers raced over the keyboard, drumming out my Facebook login info. I only had a few minutes to check notifications...

Bleep. A chat box with Darren Henderson popped up.

Darren: hey miss candace! what's up?

Wow, hadn't heard anything about that kid since the good ol' days in 4-H when I was a club manager. I didn't have time to chat, but how rude was it to ignore? I should have put my chat offline.

Candace: Just getting ready for a meeting. What are you up to these days?

Darren: i'm in iraq

His words were like pressing the shutter button of a

camera. I was the still image for five seconds.

Candace: WHAT?!

Darren: i'm a police officer in the air force

Candace: Okay, seriously, I didn't even know you were in the military!

Candace: Wow, how long have you been over there?

Darren: almost a year. i come home in january

I sat immobile. What could I say to someone who was protecting the freedom of our country? My freedom?

Candace: What's it like? Is anything the news media says true?

Darren: lol, i don't know, we don't watch it much. what are they saying?

Candace: Nothing important. What made you decide to join?

Darren: idk, to do something different. an adventure. it's a little more than i thought. man, it's hot!

Candace: haha, I'll bet. Texas summers had to prepare you some though ;-)

Darren: yeh, but not really. the sand gets in everything!

Candace: So what exactly do you do?

Darren: i patrol the base and keep everyone in line

Candace: lol, who keeps you in line?

Darren: i keep myself in line

Candace: true. I always said you were responsible.

Darren: i've lost like 20 pounds since i joined. have you seen my pics on here?

Candace: not yet. Hang on, my computer's freezing up

Candace: okay, it's going now

Candace: dude! What's with the tattoo?

Darren: lol

Candace: So, do you need anything?

Darren: well, i could always use some snacks, magazines. stuff like that.

Candace: what address do I send them to?

A few seconds passed before Darren posted the address which I copied into a Word doc and saved. Magazine titles rolled around in my head. He always talked about hunting and fishing…

Darren: how is everyone there? any small town excitement?

Candace: haha, you know us, a regular party town. County Fair just ended, made me think of all the good times we had in 4-H.

Darren: yeah that seems like a lifetime ago

Candace: man, I just can't believe you're in Iraq! Must be tough—I couldn't imagine

Darren: yeah, it's kinda hard sometimes. a friend of mine was killed by a roadside bomb a few weeks ago. you just learn to move on

Candace: I'm so sorry to hear that. You take care of yourself!

Darren: i do

I swallowed down the lump rising with my tears, glad this wasn't a phone conversation.

Darren. He still seemed like a kid to me. And a good kid. I couldn't be prouder.

Darren: well, i gotta go. time to eat and stuff

Candace: Okay, it was awesome chatting with you! Hey Darren?

Darren: yeah?

Candace: thanks for your service. I'm proud of you. We all are

Candace: We'll be praying for you!

Darren: thanks! can't wait to see everyone when i get home!

Candace: us too! Take care of yourself

Darren: thanks for chatting with me. bye!

Candace: see ya soon

Darren is offline.

A moment passed before I took a breath, thankful I hadn't missed this opportunity by putting my chat offline. Even if it made me a few minutes late to a meeting.

I clicked on the document with Darren's address and added a list:

Snacks (hearty)
Magazines (hunting, fishing)
Bible
Thank you card

A few days later, I took Darren's box to the post office. They sent me home with an extra form to fill out. Everything finally in order, it shipped. I wondered how long it might take to reach him, and hoped it made it safely. I hoped he was safe.

~~~

A month later the notification from Facebook appeared.
Darren Henderson wrote on your wall:
hey miss candace! thanks so much for the box!!! so awesome!!!!! can't wait to see y'all!!!!!!!!!

Like.

Author's note: This story is based on an actual Facebook chat with a US soldier serving in Iraq.

I am with you always. Matthew 28:20

Mustard Seed Walk

When Evil Comes

They conducted illegal experiments on my brain for three consecutive days. I fought the battle in there, praying, praying. Over and over I said, *I renounce this in the name of Jesus and by the power of His blood.* But the words never came out. They were in my heart I guess. For sure in my mind, the words the only thing blocking the experiments. The only thing saving my soul.

But things were tangling, twisting together. I could hardly remember the words anymore. I was weakening and felt my spirit leave my body. I drifted down. Or maybe up, toward heaven. I couldn't tell. A fine mist settled around me in the darkness where I stood.

This was not heaven.

A man was next to me in the garb of a biblical warrior. He stood as though ready for battle, but not against me. The shout of evil voices sounded in the distance.

"I am Michael," the man said.

I nodded. It felt as if I knew him. He handed me a sword and it was then I realized I was in full battle gear: helmet, breastplate, shield at my feet along with a broken sword. My spirit was tired. The voices came closer.

"We must fight." Michael looked ready, a strong body and determined face. "If your spirit dies, your whole being will. Fight."

I didn't have the strength to nod. They'd beaten me low. Too low. I let the tip of the new sword rest in the dirt, the hilt limp in my fingers. "I already have. I can't anymore."

Michael lifted his sword. "You've never fought alone." He turned to meet the chaotic voices. As the shapes took form, the twisted face of the chief scientist appeared—or at least a semblance of him. His spirit's ugliness was overwhelming and chilled my spirit all the way back to my soul.

I was back in my body. *I renounce this...I renounce in the name...Jesus, help me...*

The clash of swords snapped my spirit back to the darkness and the mist. Michael had stopped the scientist from skewering me, but others jumped from the shadows all around me. Training kicked in. I lifted my sword and swung in a circle, cutting air and apparitions. They screamed and retreated. Michael stayed fully engaged with the most evil of all, the main attack while I fought the flank battles.

Bloody sweat dripped down my forehead. The attacks were overwhelming. And still they came. I stumbled on the marsh-like terrain and gasped. Michael disengaged long enough to save me from a deadly blow, but shouted, "Fight! You must not surrender!"

His words sent a lightning bolt through me. It shocked and

recharged my spirit enough for me to fight on. And on. And on. The battle continued, the evilness not retreating, until at last, it began to rain. A gentle rain, nothing terrible or threatening. Not to me and Michael. But from the evil ones it elicited screams of frustration and they retreated.

The rain washed the bloody sweat from my eyes. It quenched the thirst in my parched tongue. It soothed the hot ache of my limbs. I dropped to my knees, sword in the mud beside me. I looked up at Michael. "Will they come again?"

Michael sheaved his sword. "No. Your prayers prevailed."

The mist faded and the darkness lightened. I was drifting down. Or maybe up, toward heaven. I couldn't tell.

~~~

I opened my eyes and saw my mother. She gasped, tears in her eyes as she leaned over my hospital bed. "Shhh, it's all right. You're safe. They rescued you. It may take time before you..." Her gaze questioned me, probed my mind for signs of intelligent life.

I smiled, or at least tried. "We won."

The Child

*I*t's my fault. Sharon concentrated on the math problems, her eyes turning to water when Mom started yelling into the phone.

"What's wrong with you?" Mom pressed the phone closer to her ear. "Sharon's last assignment and it's due tomorrow! How could you just leave it lying on the kitchen counter?"

Seven times eight is fifty-six. Eight hundred and sixteen minus three hundred twenty-four is...

"Are you kidding? Even if we met in the middle, it'd be late when Sharon and I got back, and I have to go to work in the morning. You need to bring it here; I don't care how long that puts you on the road!"

In front of her on the kitchen table, the half-full glass of milk lured Sharon to glance up long enough to take a sip. Mom was rolling her eyes.

"Fine then. I'll just stack this with all your other violations of the court orders, and Sharon gets a bad grade!" The phone slammed on the receiver.

One hundred and twenty divided by three is…

Sharon peeked through her long lashes. Mom stood in front of her.

"Sweetheart, I know it's hard going back and forth to your dad's house, but you must remember to bring everything back, especially homework assignments. Okay?"

Sharon nodded and a tear slipped off her chin, blotching out her division problem.

~~~

36 Years Later

"Your Honor? Sorry to bother you, but the child's attorney finally arrived. Here are the recommendation papers."

Sharon raised her head and smiled at her assistant. "Thanks, Charles. We'll reconvene in twenty minutes."

As the door to her chambers closed behind Charles, Sharon thumbed the thin folder. In twenty minutes, she would sign a decree turning a child's life upside down. Two sets of friends, two sets of pets, two bedrooms, and two parents who put the child in the middle of their petty disputes. Dad's house or Mom's house. No home.

Sharon bowed her head again and returned to prayer. *Father, what can I do? How can I make this husband and wife understand? You guided me to this place, this position of power. Why am I so powerless to make a real difference?*

Silence echoed in Sharon's ears. She opened her eyes and scanned for the expected recommended care and conservatorship of the child. But as she read, Sharon shook her head. "Are they serious? I've never decreed anything like this before."

A picture unveiled in her mind. A smile made its way to her lips, and she raised her eyebrows. Could this be a revelation?

~~~

"All rise. The court of the honorable Judge Sharon McKinley is now in session."

Sharon banged her gavel. "I've reviewed the case of Carter vs. Carter. As there are no claims of domestic violence and the reason given is incompatibility, I was prepared to sign the decree of divorce. My final decision pended the recommendation of the child's attorney regarding the minor in this case, Diana Carter."

Sharon gazed down at the husband and wife who stood separated by more than lawyers.

"I know you're going through personal trauma. You were joined as one in holy matrimony in the sight of God and man. You're about to tear yourselves in half. That's your choice. But I want to focus on the one suffering most: your daughter. You want me to declare she can no longer have a home, and disrupt her life every week, shuffling her back and forth. In lieu of this, I've decided to implement the recommendation of the child's attorney."

The courtroom filled with whispers. Sharon tapped the gavel and held up the papers in her other hand. "Jackie Shelton, the child's maternal grandmother, offered to take up residence in the couple's current home for a six month trial period. Michael and Helen Carter, you will alternately live there and care for your daughter every other week. You will exchange house keys on Thursdays at 6 P.M."

Expressions around the courtroom held confusion. The Carters' attorneys objected. Sharon banged her gavel.

"Only after the trial period will I review the Carter vs. Carter case. Court adjourned."

A final rap of her gavel stunned the room. The people rose mechanically as Sharon retired to her private quarters.

Wiping a tear from her cheek, Sharon whispered, "It's in Your hands, Father."

Life and Death Decision

Anita held her husband's hand a little tighter, willing for a twitch, a blink, some sign of intelligent life. The doctor had left moments ago, leaving her with the decision.

Funds depleted. Insurance coverage dropped. Time was winning.

How much was a human life worth? How much was Tom's life worth? Anita's stomach churned, but she hadn't eaten today so there was nothing to upchuck. Beams from the setting sun sprinkled light on the fairy-like particles in the sterile room, belittling the nausea overwhelming her.

A beep sounded, signaling low fluid levels. The beep would sound every three minutes until the nurse came in to change the bags. Actually, this machine was a little slower than some of the others. It would beep every three minutes and eight seconds. Anita had timed it earlier when she was sitting in the chair with nothing to do and too tired to press the buzzer to hurry the nurse along. She didn't want to pressure any of them anyway. The nurses had taken excellent care of her brain-dead husband the past two months. Two months too long.

Immediately after the accident, everyone told Anita it would be okay and they would make it through. Then close friends and family reassured her. Finally, it was just her.

The doctor had put it kindly, but clearly. In so many words he'd said, *this is it. Your life savings are gone, the insurance won't cover anymore once I submit my latest report. If you want to keep this up, you'll have to move him to another facility if you can afford it on your current salary. When you're working that is, not spending every waking moment by your husband's side.*

Okay, the last words Anita added herself. What people didn't understand was the part about "keep this up" referred to keeping Tom breathing artificially with the hope of him reviving someday. Of twitching, of blinking, of giving the sign of intelligent life Anita watched for now.

His skin was so changed from two months ago. The slight gray flecks over his ears that she'd teased him about days before the accident now hovered over the blotchy skin of his sagging lob. Her eyes traveled down to his pale lips, gapped open slightly, as if wanting to allow a taste of real air inside his body. His eyes…she saw them today when the doctor lifted each lid for a look. It was unnerving to see the blue eyes that once looked deep into hers now sunk in and hollow.

She rubbed her thumb over the back of his hand. She'd never felt it so soft. He had rejoiced in his carpentry work and never came in the house without bits of sawdust clinging to his clothes and hair.

The fluid monitor beeped again. Hot bile formed in the

back of Anita's throat and she let out a half scream, half growl. "Why? Why! What right do humans have to make the decision about life and death? Sure, doc, pull the plug. I don't love him enough to sit here for one more day or a hundred. Or no, I want to let him lay here and suffer just a little longer, even though everyone knows he's not coming back. But he still might." She bowed her head, choking on the saliva built up in her throat. "Jesus, what am I supposed to do?" When she realized she's prayed out loud, Anita hissed, "What am I supposed to do? Why didn't You just take him or heal him? One thing or the other, but let it be. Don't make it my decision!"

As Anita gasped for air and swallowed down her tears, something settled in her burning chest. It spread warmth and for a moment, she wondered if, at age thirty-eight, she would have a heart attack and beat Tom to the pearly gates. It was a few moments before she realized what it was. Her breathing slowed.

Peace.

It settled in her heart. After a several minutes, Anita lifted the back of Tom's hand to her lips and pressed it close. *Till death do us part.*

The door opened and Nurse Bailey came in. "Sorry about that alarm. Got caught with a patient down the hall."

Anita kept her head bowed and tried to form words, but they came out a jumbled whisper. She knew Bailey hadn't heard, so she raised her head slightly. "Would you ask the doctor to come back in here after his rounds? I've made the decision."

Letters

Familiar handwriting on the envelope stopped Lois cold. This letter was from Chloe, postmarked two days prior. The rest of the mail tumbled to the floor.

Her trembling fingers made a jagged rip in the flap. As if removing a sacred relic, she withdrew the single white sheet and unfolded it. The envelope drifted to the floor as her hand sought the nearest chair.

The words were barely legible.

Dear Ms. Lois,

By the time you read this, you should have heard that I'm dead. Don't feel bad, you did all you could. You're a nice neighbor and that's why I wanted to write you this letter.

You listened to me scream frustrations when my parents wouldn't listen to me say, "I love you." It doesn't matter now.

I'm not saying everything here. That stuff I'm saving for the note my parents will find when they find me. Not that they'll care then.

Thanks anyway.
Chloe

Lois dropped the letter as sobs boiled up to choke her. Several minutes elapsed before she could focus her eyes again. The letter stared up at her, condemning. It attested to where she had failed.

Turning her face to the ceiling, her squeaky voice etched the questions.

"God, why did you bring Chloe into my life? So I could watch hers destroyed? What more could I have done?"

The replying silence condemned her more than the letter scratched out on notebook paper. Deep inside, Lois knew. She had not done everything. She'd held back the most secret part of her soul.

~~~

Two hours later, Lois still stared at the blank sheet of stationery. The French swirls across the corner mirrored the waves in her brain.

"Just start," she murmured to herself. "Dear God, you know I can't do this." Lois closed her eyes, bit her lip. Three deep breaths.

"I can do this. I have to, for Chloe."

Dear Chloe,

With the first words written, Lois dared not pause. She had to tell the story. The image of Chloe lying in the hospital bed, IVs pumping life through her, drove the darkest moment of Lois' life into the light.

You're not alone. You're not the first. When I was nineteen years old, I attempted suicide.

The pen slipped between her fingers. She gripped harder.

I never told you of my experience because I was ashamed. No one in my life now knows of my past. I vowed to keep it that way.

If I had told you this is how I came to know the Lord, and it's what brought me to this place of joy, hope, and peace today, things might be different for you now. But that, as with all things, is past. There is a future for you, dear one. With the Lord's help, we'll face it together.

Love,

Lois

Her confession might give Chloe more questions than answers, and the prospect of discussing her own horrendous childhood made Lois sick. But could Chloe heal without it?

A gentle air of relief tingled her spine. This letter would be waiting for Chloe when she recovered.

Why Me?

The opening strains of the movie's music vibrated his eardrums. Robert slouched in his seat, arm sliding around Trina. She fit in his shoulder like God had created her just for him. Nothing more perfect than this…

"Ayah! Ah!"

Mutters followed the exclamations echoing from the middle of row sixteen. Robert must have reacted because Trina tensed. Determined, he focused on the opening sequence of the screeching car chase.

"Wahay!"

The outburst was louder, drawing *shhh's* from the surrounding seats.

"It's no big deal." Trina's breath tickled his ear. He concentrated on the intense scene. Sirens blared over the surround sound as the chase continued. The lead car shot over a cliff…

"Aho!"

Robert suppressed the hissing *shhh* crowding his throat. Why did people act like they were watching the movie at home? Whatever happened to old-fashion human courtesy?

He succumbed to the urge of turning his head as a figure jostled across the row toward them. A choking noise emitted from the small frame as he stumbled over Robert's feet. Robert avoided looking, but the sounds echoing up the main aisle caused him to shift in his seat.

Go. The quiet voice nudged him.

Why me?

Why not you?

"Be right back," he muttered in Trina's ear, already halfway to his feet.

He pushed open the door and entered the lobby, his eyes scanning the room. It was vacant with exception to the short lines at the concession area, everyone enjoying themselves in the multiplex. Everyone but him. He approached the side of the concession counter where a teen scooped popcorn into a line of jumbo buckets.

"Excuse me. A person just ran out this entrance, did you see where he went?"

Not looking up, the teen nodded toward the men's room. "A kid just ran in there."

Inside, Robert paused a moment to let his eyes adjust to the brighter light. A boy faced the opposite wall, poking it with one finger. Robert cleared his throat. "Hey, are you okay?"

The boy turned to Robert, head jerking to one side.

"Leave me alone."

In spite of the curt words, Robert saw the quiver of lip and the wet streaks on the boy's cheeks.

Why me, God?

Robert frowned. "Just thought I'd see if you were alright. Sounded like you were choking when you ran out a minute ago."

The boy reached out and poked Robert's chest three times. "Just leave me alone, okay?"

Robert guessed the boy's age at no more than thirteen, but the blue eyes tinted with fiery red suggested most of those years had been filled with anger. Robert suppressed his own agitation, and studied the boy's face. Something not quite right.

"Ayah!"

The outburst ricocheted off the walls. The boy turned away and slammed his fist into the hand dryer.

Robert shook his head and puffed a breath. "My name's Robert. What's yours?"

"Alan."

The reply cut short. They shared the mutual feeling of not wanting to talk, but Robert's choices were limited.

He recalled a TV show he'd seen recently.

"Alan, you have Tourettes Syndrome, don't you?"

A snort sounded as Alan faced him with a smile laced in sarcasm.

"How'd you guess, Columbo?"

Okay, Lord, You're leading in this. What now? I have nothing profound to say. I don't even know anything about the syndrome other than what I've seen on TV. You've got the wrong guy here, God.

"I guess that gets pretty frustrating." *Nice. See, God? What a home run.*

A home run. Robert's mind locked on the thought. "When I was growing up, all I wanted to do was play for the Boston Red Sox." Alan's stare cut through him. Robert either needed to talk fast or walk away now.

"I played my heart out. Never made many friends, just focused on my dream. But no scouts approached me my senior year. One coach finally said I just didn't have what it takes to play professionally."

Alan stared over Robert's head, but he concentrated on the words. Thoughts worked in his mind.

"Did you?"

The conversation turned close to home, curving near deep feelings. Robert had released much from his past. Still, staring it in the face again was—tough.

Robert met Alan's eyes. "No, I never played again. Others convinced me to give up. And since baseball was my life, I didn't have anything left. Nothing. I was angry at the world for a very long time."

He paused, breaking eye contact with the boy. He waited for the old burn. He sighed and smiled. No pain. No anger.

"I met a guy at the gym who shared his faith with me. He introduced me to Jesus Christ. My life hasn't been the same. Not saying I'm perfect, but my rage is gone. I got into youth baseball as a coach, and I can't imagine a better career. I married the most wonderful woman in the world. I still have my share of struggles, but now I have the Lord to see me through.

"God loves you, Alan. If you let Him, He will bring joy and peace into your life. All you have to do is ask."

The boy's eyes held on to the doubt, the pain. Robert had stared at the same kind of look in the mirror often enough.

"Our church is having a movie night next Saturday. Maybe you and your parents could come."

Alan poked at Robert again with his finger. "My parents don't like taking me anywhere. It embarrasses them when I yell and stuff."

Robert's jaw shifted but his voice stayed even when he stilled Alan's hand with a gentle grip and asked, "Where would you like to go?"

"Someplace my yelling won't bother people."

~~~

Two weeks after meeting, Alan stood cheering with Robert and Trina as the Boston Red Sox won their first game of the season.

I'd Rather Die

"I'd rather die, and be with Jesus Christ, my Savior."

I stare at Janie, horrorstruck. Her words are still floating through the air as the man lifts the gun to her face. My eyes don't close before the trigger is pulled.

A heartbeat, a skipped breath, but no tears. The shock numbs me.

When I do close my eyes, all I can see is Janie's smiling face and the years spent with my best friend. We were as close as sisters—no, closer. Never a disagreement, never an argument. Yet I wonder if Janie could understand my overwhelming fears and doubts in this moment.

I inhale and choke on the gun smoke filling the box-like room. The line moves forward.

"Deny your Jesus and live."

The woman ducks her head. Her reply is soft.

"Louder!"

"Okay, I—just…please let me go."

The gun motions her past. The line moves forward.

I don't want to die. I want to see my family again—my children. What would they choose? What do I want them to choose? When will they be brought here to make this decision?

"Deny your Jesus and live."

Another leaves unharmed. The line moves forward.

My mind buzzes. As often as this fear has come to me in the past, I didn't bring it to mind this morning. I guess I never wanted to believe it would come. Knowing Janie, she probably prepared with prayer or something before she left for our weekly chat at the coffee shop.

The men in gray coats had met us on the sidewalk and asked, "Do you claim to be a Christian?" Janie's reply was immediate and unashamed. I never answered, just nodded.

"Deny your Jesus and live."

The report of gunfire echoes seconds later. Gasps and screams shudder through the white-walled room. Moments later, the line moves forward. I taste the metallic smoke, its sting watering my eyes.

Do I really believe in Jesus? Yes, I know that without a doubt. Can I say that to the muzzle of a gun? My palms turn clammy. My kids. My husband. I can't leave them.

A dozen scriptures sweep through my soul, but I tune them out. Janie is dead. I will be, too, if I profess my faith.

"Deny your Jesus and live."

Another lives. The line moves forward.

Janie. How had she done it? Did Jesus come for her?

She had no children as I do. Maybe that was why she so freely answered the call. Had died. I don't want to die.

"Deny your Jesus and live."

As they free the man, the line moves forward. I am next.

"Deny your Jesus and live."

I stare at the floor stained with Janie's blood, then at the wall behind the gray pants and black boots. I look at the muzzle of the gun. Finally, I meet the eyes of the one who holds it. They are cold. No life behind them.

The words come with a smoothness I've never possessed. "God loves you."

"Deny your Jesus and live!"

My knees almost buckle, but a sweet presence surrounds me. "I'd rather die and be with Jesus Christ, my Savior."

A blazing light shines through to my soul. I see Him coming for me.

The gun levels on my face. I fall into the arms of my Lord Jesus.

Special Thanks

I consider my Lord Jesus Christ as the Author, I transcribe. Please direct any fan mail to Him.

That said, the task of publishing a book cannot be undertaken alone. It's not one I would consider without my world of support, physical and online. I'm surrounded with wisdom, knowledge, and encouragement everywhere I turn.

I must begin with my editor, proofreader, marketing consultant, funder, encourager…yes, I am referring to one person. My mama, Lynda Kay Sawyer. This book is as much hers as mine. I love you.

On August 26, 2012, my soul was torn when my daddy, Ara C. Sawyer, went on to be with Jesus. He dreamed of my having a log cabin to write in someday, close to a lake where he could go fishing. I know he's experiencing far greater dreams now. His life and encouragement kept me moving forward on this project. Love you, Pops. Just so you know, watching old westerns with you helped me study character development and overused storylines.

Thank you to my five brothers and their families—you've all encouraged me in different ways.

Rachel Phelps, my second editor, and a masterful writer. Thanks for the wonderful critique.

My dear, honest writing friend, Kelly Blanchard. Thank you.

To all my family and friends—This is the scary part, because I don't want to miss anyone. But just know you have a place in my heart and sincerest thanks for your encouraging words that fuel me emotionally.

To FaithWriters.com and my family there. Hats off and bookoos of love! Most of these short stories were a result of the Weekly Writing Challenge that tested and honed my writing skills month after month. Hundreds of encouraging comments and critiques from the lovely FaithWriters' members kept me going and growing. Thank you all!

To the Garden Valley Writers Group—red, blue, black pens, it doesn't matter. You taught me things I should have known about writing and didn't. Y'all rock!

Christian Writers Gathering—I founded this group as a support for local writers. For my career, the group has fulfilled its mission!

Joel Friedlander, a great big thanks for The Book Designer Blog.

Last but one of the greatest, thanks to Josh McBride, graphic designer (josh360.com) and patient friend. You're a sanity saver when it comes to technical conundrums. Thanks for the amazing cover.

ABOUT THE AUTHOR

As an inspirational author and Choctaw storyteller, Sarah Elisabeth Sawyer's mission is excellence in Christian media. She has authored over fifty inspirational flash fiction (short, short) stories. *Apparently So* won the FaithWriters.com Writing Challenge, and nine others received an Editor's Choice Award.

In 2012, she was honored as one of four artists in the Smithsonian's National Museum of the American Indian Artist Leadership Program for her literary work in preserving Trail of Tears stories.

A regular columnist in Book Fun Magazine and the Northeast Texan, she writes from her hometown in East Texas.

Also by Sarah Elisabeth Sawyer:

Touch My Tears: Tales from the Trail of Tears
For this collection of short stories, Choctaw authors from five U.S. states come together to present a part of their ancestors' journey, a way to honor those who walked the trail for their future. These stories not only capture a history and a culture, but the spirit, faith, and resilience of the Choctaw people.
Tears of sadness. Tears of joy. Touch and experience them.
Touch My Tears is available on Amazon.com

Visit her blog to watch the short film based on *Colors*:
www.sarahelisabethwrites.com/videos

www.ingramcontent.com/pod-product-compliance
Lightning Source LLC
Chambersburg PA
CBHW050529260626
47157CB00004B/1536